The Camaro and the BMW with the canted headlight were the only cars on the street she'd just taken. The other car was sixty yards behind her. In her rear-view mirror she could see the outline of the two men in the front seat. Millie braked, slowly pulled over to the curb. So did the other car.

"Why're you stopping, dear?" Mary Mike said. "Two more blocks, then take a right. She has a big two-story white house, really nice. Steve told me that Lydia paid a fortune for it."

"I know where we are, M. I just want to give you a heads-up. Tighten your seatbelt. Somebody's been following us."

"What? How can that be, Millie?" she said. Mary Mike turned to look back.

"I don't know. I'll figure that out later," Millie said. "There's a pistol in the glove compartment. Get it out and rack one into the chamber. Do you know how?" Millie pulled her Glock from its holster on her hip and a silencer from the magnetic holder under the dash. She screwed on the silencer. The Camaro's engine was still running. Headlights on.

"Jesus, Mary, and Joseph," Mary Mike said. "I haven't shot a gun in years! Hardly ever used them in the field. God help me, I preferred needles." She opened the glove compartment and pulled out a Glock 27, a smaller, more compact model than Millie's 22.

"Maybe you're wrong," she said. "Why would any-one follow us?"

"Why? Are you kidding? I've just whacked two Russian hitters, and by now half the Russian gangsters in Boston probably know that we're looking for Yuri Kuznetsov. Any other questions?"

"If you're right, they'll try to kill us, won't they?" Speaking matter-of-factly, not afraid.

"Probably."

Mary Mike checked the load in the magazine, popped it back in. Chambered a round like an expert. Just like bicycle riding—you never forget.

"OK, M, hang on--let's see if those bozos know how to play," Millie said. She threw the car into gear, floored the gas pedal, and the Camaro, whipping its tail back and forth, bolted forward.

DEAD
SURE

DEAD SURE

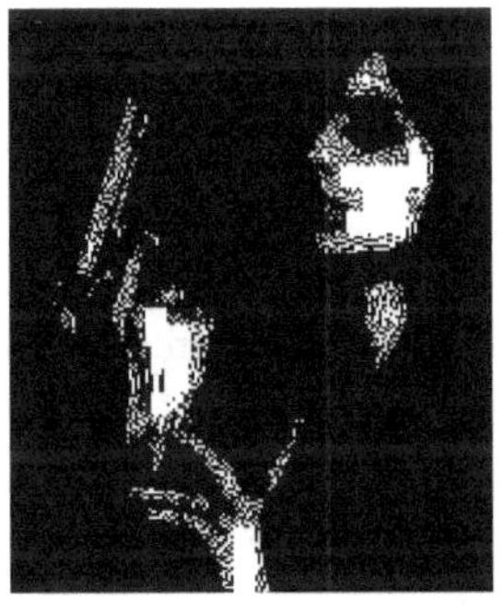

Jerry Masinton

Anamcara Press LLC

Published in 2024 by Anamcara Press LLC
Author © 2024 Jerry Masinton
Illustrations © 2023 by ©Volodymyr Shcerbak - stock.adobe.com
Book design by Maureen Carroll
Georgia, Timeburner, and Salvation.

Printed in the United States of America.
Book Description: In this humorous crime spoof, a contract killing takes a deadly turn when a supposedly dead Russian mobster
resurfaces at his own funeral. As bullets fly in a church, Millie finds
herself in a dangerous game involving fake nuns, hidden agendas,
and a web of deception.

ANAMCARA PRESS LLC
P.O. Box 442072, Lawrence, KS 66044

https://anamcara-press.com/

Ordering Information:
Quantity sales. Special discounts are available on quantity purchases
by corporations, associations, and others. For details, contact the
publisher at the address above.
Orders by U.S. trade bookstores and wholesalers. Please contact
Ingram Distribution.

Publisher's Cataloging-in-Publication data
Masinton, Jerry, Author
Dead Sure / Jerry Masinton

[1. FIC050000   Fiction / Crime . 2. FIC060000   FICTION / Humor-
ous / Black Humor. 3. FIC062000   FICTION / Noir.]
ISBN-13: 978-1-960462-30-5 (Paperback)
ISBN-13: 978-1-960462-29-9 (EBook)

Library of Congress Control Number: 2024932729

Dedication

For Dick, my brother and most enthusiastic reader.

Contents

WhatThe truly unique trait of sapiens is
our ability to create and believe fiction.
All other animals use their communication
system to describe reality. We use our
communication system to create
new realities.

–Yuval Noah Harari

Chapter 1

Sheila's Rule

Monday Morning, October 3, 11:00

It had started out as a simple hit. Millie had a contract to whack one guy in Kansas City—that was it. But things got complicated, one thing led to another, and before you know it she'd had to take out two guys in Des Moines, three in Brooklyn, and one more in Kansas City.

Now Millie was wrapping up the postmortem on the Kansas City job with Ralph and Mary Mike. They were sitting in Ralph's kitchen at the antique oak table that he had inherited from Sheila, his late mother. She had also willed him her share of the business, Continental Removals. They were drinking coffee and eating Dippin' Donuts, their meal of choice for postmortems.

Millie liked the postmortems—coffee and donuts in the morning, Dagwood sandwiches at noon, a hit or two of Jack Daniel's Black or Buffalo Trace an hour or two later to stay on keel.

Ralph was wearing khakis with black suspenders, a long-sleeved pink Oxford button-down, and black silk socks with pink flamingos circling his ankles. The ensemble was completed with black slides from Nike for that crucial touch of cool.

"Seven bodies on this job, Millie," Ralph said. "And we started out with just a contract on one fuckin' guy—Sheldon Kukich."

"Eight, if you count Jauncey's friend Lionel," Millie said, "but it was Jimmy Twist who actually iced him, if you remember."

"Oh, yeah, the one in the bar. You broke his finger."

"Um-hmm, that one. Lionel."

"Still, a lot of dead guys," he said, "and a lot of snags. I don't see how you figured it all out."

"I just followed the bread crumbs, Ralphie."

"What? What bread crumbs?"

"Just an expression, Ralphie."

Bright light from the outdoors poured in through the windows. The tall trees in the yard and Ralph's indoor plants gave the room a homey feel. Life is good, Millie thought.

Mary Mike stood up, stretched her arms over her head, sighed, and sat back down. She had on a full-length cotton print dress—pale blue background, neon-red and -yellow Hawaiian flowers—along with red gingham sandals. One of her favorite lounging outfits. Her long gray hair swirled counter-clockwise on her head, resembling a category 4 hurricane on the weather guy's show.

Everybody was relaxed, just a happy little family discussing business matters, dotting the i's and crossing the t's of every little detail, like making sure Ralphie knew the exact count of bodies from the previous job. Keep him up to speed.

Millie had just finished working out at Equinox, her short brown hair still damp from the shower. She was wearing skin-tight magenta and black Calvin Klein Performance tights that only an experienced forensics team could say for sure hadn't been spray-painted on her body.

"Ralphie," she said, "can you pass the donuts again? I'm starved this morning. Five miles on the treadmill, plus weights. Good thing you bought a couple of dozen. I'm deep down to the bone needy for donuts."

Ralph's phone rang. "It's Philly," he said, staring at the phone. "Huh. The hell's up?"

"Easy way to find out, Ralphie." Millie said. "Answer it."

Ralph thought about it.

"Go ahead, Ralphie, what're you waiting for?" Mary Mike said. She had been softly humming "Amazing Grace" when the phone rang. She had a pretty good voice, Millie thought. Probably sang a lot when she attended parochial schools as a kid.

The phone rang again. Kept ringing. Mary Mike looked at Millie. Millie looked back, lifted her eyebrows and shoulders a millimeter: Don't ask me.

"I was just thinking, he never calls this early—Barney."

The phone stopped ringing. Mary Mike lifted her palms, looked at Ralph with her mouth open.

"I was just getting ready to answer," Ralph said. "Maybe he made a mistake and thought it was somebody else."

"It rang five times and you just looked at it like it was a dead fish," Millie said. "What'd you expect? He'll call back." She was scoping out the platter of donuts in the middle of the table. The glazed, she thought, make sure you get one or two more before they're all gone.

"What do you think, Mary Mike?" Ralph said. "Why would he call in the morning? He never does that."

"Ralphie, hon'," she said, "what difference does it make when he calls?" She poured more coffee for herself and Millie. Ralph shook his head no.

"I don't know," he said. "It's just that Barney said somethin' I been wondering about. This was day before yesterday."

"Barney. Barney Halcovage," Mary Mike said. She reached for a Boston Kreme, broke it in two, and dunked one half.

"Yeah," Ralph said.

"Why didn't you tell us? There's not a situation, is there?"

"I don't know," Ralph said. "Maybe somethin', maybe nothin'."

"Um-hmm, that's real helpful, Ralphie," Mary Mike said. She rotated her hands impatiently. "Can you just for Jesus' sake tell us what he said?"

"Well," Ralph said, "he called me. This was in the afternoon. 'Ralph,' he said, 'I'm gonna get right down to the main point here with you. I'm not a guy that likes to beat around the bush, you understand? Some guys, you know, they bullshit about this, bullshit about that, but they never get the ball down the field.' 'Barney,' I said, 'the fuck're you getting at? Just say it.' 'Oh, yeah,' he said. 'OK. Here's the shot, Ralph—I decided, so I decided I need to get out, OK?' I thought to myself, the hell's he saying? 'The fuck're you in, that you gotta get out?' I said. 'You don't mean the outfit, do you?' Just kind of rolling with him, you know?   Kidding around. 'Yeah,' he said, 'the outfit, Ralph, the business I've been in—like what?—since with your mom, God rest her soul. All these years since then. And now, like I say, I need a little time for myself, see?'"

"Barney Halcovage," Mary Mike said. "How do you know his name? You guys're not supposed to know each other, let alone use your real names on the phone, you know that? Where did you meet him?"

"I never met him, how could I?"

"That's right, how could you? So what's going on here?" she asked. "Is this a development of some kind?" Her hair settled an inch or so over her forehead.

"Can't tell," he said. "Like I said." With both hands he smoothed the front of his pink shirt. "Why would he want out? That's why I'm telling you. And P.S., I know about not using real names because you always said not to. But it wasn't me that started the conversation."

"I see that, but still. Your mother and I," Mary Mike said, "we set up the contact system with firewalls—nobody knows anybody else. Sheila's idea, that was. A genius she was, in her chosen profession. She said, 'All of our contacts, they only have their specific numbers to call. No names, ever. That way, nobody can trace our people or the client. In the office here, of course, we know the names of the contacts in every city, which we're the only ones who do.'"

This wasn't the first time that Mary Mike had taught her history lesson. Every once in a while she decided to give a refresher course. Millie knew it by heart.

"Now, Ralphie, you mention the name of a guy we put in place a long time ago," Mary Mike said.   "And you two are using first names like you're sweethearts. But you said he didn't tell you his name, so how did you know it?"

"You mean, how do I already know his name, right?"

"Mother of God, Ralphie, it's a simple question," Mary Mike said.

"Let me ask a couple of things here," Millie said. "Ralphie, I'm hearing that this is a breach of protocol. Is that right?   Barney—did he seem rattled? It sounds like something might've skidded off-kilter for him."

"Did he mention a contract?" Mary Mike said. "That's what his job is." A hint of agitation on the horizon.

"Yes and no," Ralph said. "He heard a rumor. He had to get off the phone after a few minutes."

"A rumor," Mary Mike said. "What kind of rumor? Like, some big player wants to pay us a couple of million to take out a U.S. senator? Or a rumor like Tom Brady's gonna come back to the Patriots?" Being a little pissy about this thing, Millie thought.

"Just, he was a little nervous," Ralph said.

"A situation, then," Mary Mike said. "Why didn't you just say so right away?"

Ralph raised his shoulders. Lowered them. Lifted his eyebrows: I'm innocent.

"OK, fill out the picture," Mary Mike said. "And don't forget my blood pressure here, Ralphie. I want to know if there's any actual trouble." Her voice climbing in pitch and volume now, though not yet where the fat lady sings.

Ralph drank some coffee. "Like I said, he was a little jittery," Ralph said. "Talkin' about retirement. Why would he tell me that? Anyway, he said to me, 'Ralph, I been thinkin' here. It's like this—I been going over it in my head, and I decided I maybe oughtta get out. Take it easy, you know, make time for my other activities.'"

"He mentioned other activities?" Mary Mike said. "I don't believe it. He's like you—he doesn't have any other activities. Take it from me, Ralphie, Barney's never been what you call active. His mom told me he sits around the house all day watching TV. Long time ago, I heard, he liked Judge Judy." She turned to Millie: "Pass the donuts, hon', I want one of those crullers before you decide deep down to the bone you gotta have 'em."

"M, the crullers are all yours. I'm swearing off crullers for Lent."

"Lent was six months ago, sweetheart."

Then she said to Ralph: "He used your name, right? He just came right out and said, 'Ralph,' you're saying? That could be risky."

"That's what I been sayin'," Ralph said. "Barney said, 'Ralph, maybe it's time for me to get out and—what do they call it on Oprah?—start a new chapter. You follow me?'"

"A new chapter?" Mary Mike said. "Are you for God's sake pulling my leg, Ralphie? Who talks like that? 'A new chapter!' Is he writing a book?" No doubt about it now—Mary Mike's voice up there in the fat lady's range.

"See, that's why I didn't tell you right away," Ralph said.

"Well, at least we know that he likes Oprah now," Millie said. "What I don't get is this guy needing more time for himself. How often does he call you in a year? Ten, twelve times?"

"Yeah. You know. It depends."

"Um-hmm. And how long does each call take? Two or three minutes—five at the outside?" Millie getting into it now.

"Yeah, that's ballpark. Unless somethin' comes up."

"And once in a great while, like with our favorite Mafia poster boy, Joey D'Angeli," Millie said, "you have to call Philly back and say, 'We got a question for the client.' And then Philly calls you back and he says, 'The client won't budge. Sorry.' And that's that."

"Yeah, basically."

"Now, Ralphie, add it all up," Millie said. "In a year's time, our guy in Philly spends—what would you say?—a total of an hour or so on the phone with us? OK, maybe add in a few more minutes so he has time to think about how to punch in the numbers."

"I see where you're goin' with this," Ralph said.

"Good. I've been laying it out pretty careful for you. So I have a question."

"The question," Mary Mike said, "Millie's question is, 'Barney Halcovage doesn't spend any time as it is doing this job in the first place.'"

"So why," Millie said, "does he need time off?" She looked out the kitchen window. The sunlight was dimming slightly, giving the room a soft golden glow.

"What's he going to do with that extra hour each year, anyway?" Mary Mike said. "Why can't he write his next chapter after making a couple of calls?" Not a question.

"I get you," Ralph said, "but that's not what Barney means. Here's his deal: 'Guys get burned out after a long time on the job,' he said. 'I'm not a kid no more, likes to break balls. I'm mellowing out, these days.' Then he says, 'I gotta hang up now, Ralph. But, hey, before I forget, why I called you: I been hearing talk about a new contract in the pipeline. Something funny about a hot-shot Russian in your district, which you know I don't trust the fucking Russians. But so far I don't know no details.'"

"'So why the fuck you call me, you don't have any details?' I said.

"'I'll let you know,' he said. And that was that, period."

"So he did want to talk about a contract," Millie said. "Why didn't you just say so?" She stood up and opened the fridge. Lunch time coming up. Ralph always stocked it like a miniature deli for her.

"Because," Mary Mike said, "Ralphie didn't just want to come right out and say, 'We got a problem here.' He wanted to start slow, build it up so my head doesn't explode from high blood pressure. Am I right, Ralphie?" Her words now exploding like gunshots. Time to break out the Jack Black, Millie thought. Forget about the sandwich for now.

Ralph lifted one shoulder. Let it drop.

"Ralphie," Millie said, "Mary Mike is just checking things out, OK? You don't need to give her any attitude. She's entitled to ask a few questions, but it's just family here and she understands you were under a strain. But you did fuck up."

"Yeah, OK, OK. Forget it."

Millie could see a few clouds moving across the sun, but nothing threatening yet. It was 11:55. Millie brought three tumblers from the cabinet, along with a fresh bottle of Jack Daniel's, to the table. God bless Ralphie for keeping a good supply of bourbon on hand.

"But I have a question, M," said Millie. "It's not just using first names that kicked you into high gear, is it?

It's Barney wanting to retire. What's all that about? He won't talk, will he?"

"No, no, he'd never say a word. He's stand-up, all the way."

"So who cares?" Millie said. "Just put another guy in the Philly station. You know people. Hackers who live in dark rooms, documents guys, retired banking insiders, information brokers, tough-guy Southies. You probably have a Rolo-dex."

Mary Mike sighed. "You're right, hon'. It's Barney saying he wants out. The thing is," her voice almost intimate now, "the thing is, you don't retire from this job. Ever. Once you're in, you're in. It's Sheila's Rule. It was her idea. We never talked about it before today because the subject just never came up."

"Nope, I guess we haven't," Millie said, nodding her head. "First it was Ralphie forgetting to mention that you were in the firm when I came on board . . ."

"It just slipped my mind, Mil," Ralph said. "I didn't mean . . ."

"And now," Millie said, "now it's some kind of fucking Cosa Nostra clubhouse rule or something that says you're a lifer in the firm the minute you walk through the door, whether you like it or not. Am I getting close?" Leaning toward them, her elbows on the table, nostrils flared.

"I guess so, dear, yeah," Mary Mike said. "But I really haven't thought about the rule lately, Barney's call got my attention. Sheila and I decided at the beginning that nobody retires and decides to spend their time in bars throwing darts, drinking too much. There's good money here, but no retirement plan. You got lifetime security—look at it that way. See, hon', we can't have a bunch of retirees out in the world, maybe deciding to free-lance now and then, begging to be compromised. It's a security issue. Does that bother you?"

"I'll let you know, M," Millie said, nodding her head

again. "It's something to think about. Has anybody besides Barney ever tried to leave the business?" She put a couple of glazed donuts on her plate.

"Now that you mention it, yeah," Ralph said. "But only one guy. Remember that retired grade-school teacher I told you about, first or second time we talked? Guy who was our mechanic for a while to fatten up his pension? He decided he wanted out one day when he was on a job."

"Sure, I remember. He ended up shot and tossed into a dumpster in Fall River. Occupational hazard, you called it. You told me he didn't have a good sense of humor, either. Now I can see why. So you arranged a hit on him."

"Millie—Mil—we're not fuckin' animals," Ralph said, his shoulders up by his ears, his eyes squeezed shut.

"So who took him out—the target?" Millie said. "The target got wise and flipped the game on your shooter?"

"No, no, I don't know what happened to the target. We never found out. He just disappeared. Never seen anything like it. Somebody got past our guy's cover, but it wasn't the target. That deal cost us a lot of fuckin' money, by the way."

"I know. You told me, more than once," Millie said. "So either some random killer took out your guy or he shot himself in the head and jumped into the dumpster, right?" she said.

"Huh-uh. It's kinda complicated, Mil." Ralph with the shoulders again, plus a big frown this time. A lot of body language today, Millie thought.

"You know, this morning I woke up and had the feeling that everything made sense," Millie said. "You ever do that, Ralphie? Wake up and think, 'It all adds up if you just pay a little fucking attention to the details'?"

"Hell, I don't know, Mil. What difference does it make, what I think?"

"She means," Mary Mike said, "that you'd better tell

her what happened to our hitter. Because so far you haven't explained a lot."

"It gets better and better," Millie said. "Why haven't we had this nice little conversation before now? I'm a big girl. I don't faint at the sight of blood."

"The reason, hon'," Mary Mike said, "is because it's just something that happened a long time ago, like a bad traffic accident, and we're always busy with a new contract or you're out in the field or something and until Barney talked 'retirement,' I put it out of my head."

"I want a drink," Ralph said. "It's past noon. We can start."

Millie poured half a fist of Jack Black into each of the three tumblers. Mary Mike and Ralph each took a big slug of the whiskey. Millie sipped hers, savoring the woody, sweet aroma that started in her nose and carried its burn all the way down inside.

Ralph and Mary Mike sat without moving, staring down at their tumblers. Not a sound in the room.

"OK," Millie said, "this is what I want to know: What the hell good is Sheila's Rule if you don't enforce it?"

"If you want the truth," Mary Mike said, "we don't talk about it anymore. But in this business people can't just up and leave. This isn't Sears—you want to move on to something else, you give the company as a reference." She sounded like a union boss, Millie thought. "What do you think, dear?"

Millie shook her head slowly.

"Here's what I think: I think that your shooter bumped up against Sheila's Rule in Fall River and it got him killed," she said. "I also think it's high fucking time for you guys to explain what happened."

She poured more Jack Daniel's into their glasses.

Chapter 2

Marco di Marco

A Few Minutes Later

Ralph and Mary Mike were on their third or fourth drink. Millie had no intention of keeping up. She was looking in Ralph's fridge for a bottle of Sam Adams to go with her sandwich.

"The guy," Ralph said, "—Eddie Deakin his name was—he wasn't a bad shooter." Ralph finally getting around to telling what had happened to the schoolteacher. "He was slow but, you know, real careful. Planned everything out, down to the last fuckin' detail."

"That usually keeps you alive," Millie said, "careful planning." She found cello-packed lunch meats, sliced cheeses, a jar of Kalamata olives, half a pound of Genoa salami in butcher wrap, the hand-made kind. Also a six-pack of Rolling Rock to go with the Sam Adams: Ralphie venturing into new territory.

"Yeah, OK, but who knows in this case? Somebody popped him and it was only by chance that the guy we hired to do the job that the schoolteacher decided he didn't want to do—that the second guy found him."

Ralph explaining things.

"Jesus, Ralphie." Millie here.

"Yeah, I know, people outside the business, they think it's simple. Just follow a guy, pop him, and drive home. But not everybody's cut out for this type job."

"That's not what she means, Ralphie," Mary Mike said. "What you're saying here is already tangled up, and you've just started the story."

"Have I lost you, Mil?" Ralph said.

"Huh-uh. I just meant that I can already see trouble coming. And I wondered how things got so screwed up at the very beginning. Is that a specialty of yours?" She was thinking about Ralph's mistake at the start of the Kansas City job, when he let the client, Joey Angels, make a dumb change at the last minute. Bygones, Millie, forget about it. "Just go on, I'm fine," she said.

"Oh-kay. So. Our shooter decides—this is after we sent him out, he's done his homework, he's ready to go— he calls me on the phone and says, 'Ralph, it's me, Eddie, and I got a little problem. The gentleman you want me to fix up?'

"'Yeah?' I said. 'OK,' he said, 'I practically got him in my sights,' Eddie says. 'I got his routine down pat. He's in a little bar across the street from me now and he's gonna walk home in thirty minutes, like he does every evening. He goes down a dark little side street to get to his apartment. Job's a piece of cake.'

"'Then why the hell're you calling me? Just pay him off when he gets there. You want some advice?' I said. 'Just hide in the dark so you can surprise him.'"

"'No,' he said, 'that ain't it. I know how to handle it. I'm just tellin' you it's not dangerous, so that's not the reason why I can't do it.'"

"You're telling me that he really talked that way—this schoolteacher?" Millie said.

"Of course not, hon'," Mary Mike said. "Ralphie just likes to tell it his way."

"What's the difference?" Ralph said. "I ain't makin' anything up. Who cares how you tell it if it's the truth?" Millie had heard Ralph tell a lot of stories. Mary Mike was right: He had his own style. Call it Ralph-ese, Millie thought.

"Why don't you get to the point, Ralphie?" Mary Mike said. "I'm getting hungry." Millie was too, but she wanted to hear the story.

"Yeah, OK. The guy—our boy Eddie—says to me on the phone, 'Ralph, I can't do this fucking job. I got the shakes, bad, real bad. This ain't the first time, which I don't know why they happen. Before, I just went ahead with the job. Now?—maybe it's the cold weather this year, but I'm shakin' all over. I can't even hold on to the gun. I must of caught something terrible. I'm sorry to call you, last minute, but you gotta help me, you gotta get somebody else. In fact, I can't do this work no more.'

"I could hear him breathing hard, but what the hell? He had a fuckin' job to do, and the target was practically doing it for him. Who cares if he had the shakes? I woulda liked to kill the son-of-a-bitch," Ralph said, "but all I could say is, 'Don't do this, Eddie, you can't back out. You'll regret it.'"

"'I know, I know,' he said. 'But this one's an easy job, like I say, so my replacement, he can practically call it in. I'm going back to my hotel here and climb in bed with a bottle until I get well.' And then he said, 'So long, Ralph, and thanks for everything.' Can you believe that?" Ralph said.

"And you never heard from him again." Millie said.

"Not a fuckin' word, Mil. Next thing I know, he's in the dumpster with a bullet hole between his eyes. It's spooky, like I whacked him just by thinking about it. But he put me in a jam. I hadda call in a hitter the last minute, which you know is not professional, not to mention dangerous because of all the shit that you can't see coming. But we had an obligation to the client, and

I'm also worried about the money angle. I'm sweating bullets, in other words, because I never had to bring in a fuckin' replacement before."

"So then," Mary Mike said, "he called me—Ralphie did—and asked me who do I know from my long list of undesirable citizens who'd be willing to commit murder on a moment's notice." The whiskey seemed to be helping her skate forward with the story, Millie thought. A nice pink glow on M's broad, round cheeks, too.

"'I know one right off the bat,' I said. 'Your mom and I wanted to put him in the Albany station, when we still had plans for one. I'll call him.' Turns out Kinty Doyle's taking care of his sick mother in Poughkeepsie. So nothing doing there. But—you remember, Ralphie?—I remembered another hitter. I had to make some calls, but we finally got in touch with him, told him who the players were, and he's on the job the next day—just like that."

"You didn't have a face-to-face with him? Show him photos?" Millie said.

"Actually, no, dear, because we were in a tizzy. We should have, I know that now, looking back. But he said, 'No trouble, Mary Mike. Just give me the game plan. Little town like Fall River? Can't miss.'"

"What's his name—this guy you trusted to ID the target over the phone?"

"Marco Brabano," Mary Mike said. "Marco di Marco, we called him from the old days in parochial school, don't ask me why. Very nice kid. Came from a good family. But a little weird, too, if you want the truth. Kinda shy. He'd never done any work for us, but people talked about him."

"Jesus, Mary Mike, you were taking a big chance. Was this guy any good?" Millie wasn't thinking about her sandwich any longer.

"Well, hon', here things got sticky. He was good at one time, they say—professional all the way. Absolutely dependable. And quiet as the grave. At least he had that reputation. I'd kept his name on file."

"But he went off the tracks in Fall River," Ralphie said. "Iced the wrong guy, scared off the target, shot up the bar they were in, and we lost Eddie Deakin to boot."

"What did the police say about the mysterious dead guy in the dumpster?" Millie said.

"You got me, Mil," Ralph said. "We saw the news on TV, that's all. What could the cops say? They knew less than we did."

Millie listened as Ralph told his story, slowly running her index finger around the rim of her glass, fitting all the pieces together.

"So Marco di Marco took Deakin's place"—this is Millie a couple of minutes later—"and went to Fall River. Marco followed the target to the bar where Deakin had spotted him, charged in, and started blasting away. Not a good entry for a hit man, by the way," she said. "Then he killed a guy who may or may not have resembled the target. Am I OK so far?"

Ralph nodded his head yes.

"And for act three," Millie said, "Marco critically wounded two other patrons who had nothing to do with the action. Meanwhile, the guy with the target on his back, by this time realizing what the evening's entertainment is, parachutes out of the scene, pronto. Then, a short time later, your boy Marco di Marco delivered the good news to you about Eddie Deakin."

Millie paused a moment. "Now, have I got all this stuff right?"

"Yeah," Ralph said.

"Good, but there's a piece or two missing," she said.

"Like what?" he said.

"Like, follow the dots connecting Eddie in his hotel room, sucking on a bottle, and Eddie in the dumpster leaking blood," Millie said. "In other words, how would Marco have any idea that Eddie Deakin was in the dumpster—unless he put him there?"

"How do you figure that, Mil?" Ralph said.

"You called Marco and set it all up on the phone, gave him the names of people and places," said Millie. "You told him what Eddie had done. You must've told him where Eddie was staying, too. Why not? Eddie was a big part of the story. And Marco di Marco, the big-time pro, didn't need you to tell him in so many words, 'Eh, Marco, take-a out that son-of-a-bitch Eddie Deakin too, for letting me down.' He'd know that guys who violate the code have to be taken out."

"What code?" Ralph said.

"Jesus Christ, Ralphie," Millie said.

"She means Sheila's Rule," Mary Mike said. "But Marco was never in the firm," she said, "so he couldn't know about it. All we told him was, 'Marco, we have to move quick because of Eddie's'—what did we call it, Ralphie?—'the situation Eddie got us into.'"

"You wanted a pro, I guess you got a pro, M, just not a very good one," Millie said. "He heard what he thought you wanted him to hear: 'Take out the target, and while you're at it whack Eddie Deakin, too.' That was OK. But he didn't shoot the guy—he whacked somebody else—and then he went out and did almost everything else wrong, too. Kind of funny, if you like that kind of humor. What happened to him?"

"The guy was killed a week later in a hit-and-run," Ralph said. "We heard about it on TV. Cops never found the driver. Couldn't find the car, either. Ended up, the cops said 'gang-related' and dropped the whole thing."

"So you decided to clear the board," Millie said.

Ralph and Mary Mike glanced at each other. Uh-huh, Millie thought.

"Tell me if I'm wrong," Millie said. "After the target had vanished into thin air, there was nothing to do except refund the client's fee. But Marco di Marco was a big embarrassment to the firm. So if somebody took him out—this small-time bozo who'd iced the wrong guy in the bar and let the actual target get away—who'd give a damn? And you'd be sending a message that Continental Removals takes care of its mistakes."

"What can I say, Mil?" Ralph said.

"You can tell me what you did."

"Me? Nothing," Ralph said. "Me and Mary Mike talked it over. We knew we had to do something, but we didn't like the options. We worried for a couple of days, and then Mr. Moustakas said, 'I fix for you. You no need to worry no more.' You know how he talks. And that was that. We did our best."

"You know," Millie said, "first thing Mr. Moustakas showed me when I joined the firm was the white cargo van he uses for cleaning. I could have used it in Iraq. Bullet-proof glass, industrial cleaning supplies inside, weapons in hidden compartments. And in front he had one of those big road-armor bumpers. It took me a while to figure out why he needed that."

Chapter 3

Yuri Kuznetsov

An Hour Later, Monday, 1:30 p.m.

Ralph and Mary Mike were eating leftover Irish stew that she'd cooked the day before. Millie was enjoying the Italian hoagie that she'd started to build an hour earlier. Big deli roll, capicola, Genoa salami, provolone, rosemary- and-garlic-flavored roast beef, lettuce, tomatoes, pepperoncini. Whatever she could find. Plus an icy bottle of Sam Adams to wash it down.

No one had said a word for half an hour, not since the information that Millie had pried out of Ralph and Mary Mike re: the late and unlamented Eddie Deakin and Marco di Marco. Ralph had wandered out of the room. Now he was back reading a fall catalog for tulip bulbs. Mary Mike had stayed in the kitchen to clean up, alternately whistling and humming "Danny Boy" out of tune.

Millie walked into the living room, lay on the couch, and thought about what Mary Mike and Ralphie had told her. She saw that every event in the whole sad saga of Eddie and Marco had been triggered by Eddie's last-minute decision to quit the business. Every subsequent event was connected, every improbable action set in motion, by it—dominoes tumbling toward their inevitable end. Put it in your file, Millie, you never know when you'll need it. She returned to the kitchen.

Ralph's phone rang.

"It's from Philly," Ralph said. He stopped chewing. Looked at the phone.

"Good, Ralphie, now what's the next step?" Millie said.

"C'mon, Mil, get your boot off my throat, will ya? I'm still depressed thinking about what we were talkin' about." He picked up after the third ring. "Yeah? Yeah, Barney? Was that you earlier today? It was? Good. I was wonderin'. No, nothing. Fine. Having lunch now. How about you?"

Mary Mike circling her index finger in the air: Forget the chit-chat, move things along.

"No, I don't think so, Barn, no. Hang on." Ralph all business now.

He held the phone to his chest. "Barney wants to know, did we ever ice one of the Russians here that wiped out the Albanians. I told him . . ."

"I heard what you told him," Mary Mike said. "And I want to know why you're using first names on the line again."

"Oh yeah, sorry, but we all know who's who here today, right?"

Mary Mike lifted her arms, let them fall back to her lap. Shook her head. "I have to pee," she said. She stood up.

"By the way, Barn," Ralph said, "why did you call earlier today?"

Mary Mike turned back. "Give me the phone," she said, her tone colder than the far side of the moon. Ralph closed his eyes, handed it over to her.

The room was getting dimmer. The day getting

cloudier. Storm coming? Millie took in the little drama playing in front of her as she ate her sandwich.

"Why're you guys using first names now?" Mary Mike said. "You and our guy here making policy now? Reorganizing the business? Union working hours, casual Fridays, concealed weapons optional?" Nice use of sarcasm, Millie thought. Or is it irony?

Mary Mike listened for a few seconds. "Look, I'm not really mad, OK? But you have to be careful from now on—you and the guy on this end. It's a matter of security."

Barney said something. Mary Mike rolled her eyes and tipped her head to one side.

"No," she said, "in fact I have something else on my mind here—something more important. Are you listening?" Pause. "I'm the one who hired you to run the Philly station, remember? I'm the one who saw long-term career possibilities for you when you were a juvie. This firm depends on you, all right? So what is all this talk about retiring?" Spitting bullets again.

Barney talking again, apparently defending himself. Mary Mike drumming her fingers on the table.

"You know fucking well," she said, "that that's your job. Pardon my French. And let me remind you that you're the sole support of your mother. She depends on you. What'll she do if something happens to you? If you're out of the picture? Do you follow me?"

Barney on high volume now, Mary Mike holding the phone well away from her ear.

"No, it's just business," she said. "It has nothing to do with you. You should know that. Now zip it up on the topic of writing new chapters and smelling the roses."

Barney started to say something else. Mary Mike shook her head, looked up at the ceiling, and cut him off: "I told you I'm not mad, just a stickler for safety.

Rules are rules. And by the way, there's no Albanian mafia in Boston. Never has been. Yeah. Here's our guy."

She handed the phone back to Ralph. Her hair had fallen over one eye. With one side of her mouth, she aimed a stream of air upward and tried to blow it back into place. No luck. Millie remembered a good-looking blonde actress from the old black-and-white movies whose hair always fell over one eye. Couldn't think of her name. "My bladder's bursting," Mary Mike said.

"So what, then?" Ralph said, "You got a guy wants to put out a contract on a Russian here in Boston?"

He listened, then said, "Hang on a minute." He looked at Millie. "Can we do a rush job? That's why he called earlier today." Millie lifted her shoulders, shook her head: I don't like it.

"I'll get back to you, Barn. Meantime, see what else you can find out. Yeah. No, no, she's not pissed off." Ralph ended the call. He pushed away his half-eaten bowl of stew. Reached for the bottle of Jack Black, lifted it, gazed at it. Something in the deep-copper color of the whiskey seemed to interest him. He half-filled his tumbler. Did the same for Mary Mike's. Millie shook her head no.

Mary Mike returned from the bathroom. "I heard you say something about a Russian a minute ago. Philly has a contract on him?"

"Wait a second, all right?" Millie said. "Before we even start to talk about this Russian. The reason we haven't touched these guys in the past, we don't have the resources to take on the Russian Mafia, if that's what he is. We've gone over this before. Bad enough we got tangled up with the Italian Mafia in Brooklyn. I had to take out three of those bozos, Ralphie. Remember? I'm the one with my ass on the line out there."

"I know, Mil, but we didn't go in knowing that. And Barney says this guy's just some . . ."

"Jesus, Ralphie, you knew the client was a Mob guy in that job," Millie said. "We talked about it. You said he wouldn't take no for an answer. You didn't want to buck him. Don't try to rewrite history."

"I kinda forgot—you know, with all that went on after."

"Yeah," Millie said, "blood under the bridge. I'm going to get another beer. You guys want one?"

Ralph said, "Yeah, I need a chaser." Mary Mike didn't reply.

"Ralphie, what are the details? Can you get to the point?" Mary Mike said. "This Russian's going to die of old age before we get to him."

"Yeah, OK. So here's what he had for us. Barney. He said, 'Ralph, case anyone asks, the guy ain't connected no more, he's just a guy. We don't have to worry. Used to be somebody. But he ain't nobody now. It's just personal, see. A regular hit. You interested?' I said, 'We'll think about it.' Now see, Mil, no reason to get worked up."

"Did he give out a name?" Millie asked. "Who is this guy who used to be a big shot but now is a nobody? And why should we be called in to whack him?" She had put down her hoagie.

"Who knows? Little guys get iced all the time. Husbands, boyfriends, business partners, of course. Somebody crosses somebody."

"A name, Ralphie? Has the guy got one?"

"I never heard of him, Mil, just relax. Philly said we're gonna get double our fee for this one." He put both hands palm down on the table.

"Christ, Ralphie, we've heard that one before," Millie said. "It's a bad sign. Let's do this like pros, OK? This is a little guy, he's not important anymore, and somebody wants to pay us double to kill him? Think about it." She sucked down some Sam Adams. Rubbed the cold bottle against her forehead.

"Ralphie—the name, for god's sake?" Mary Mike said. She held her hands out wide, pushed her jaw forward, Italian style: allora? Well?

"Kuznetsov, like a sneeze," Ralph said. "First name's Yuri. Mid-fifties, late-fifties, Barney didn't know."

"Never heard of him," Millie said. "But then how many Russians do I have on speed dial?"

"Yuri Kuznetsov," Mary Mike said. "Hmm. That name rings a bell." Pause. Lifted her eyes to her forehead. Snapped her fingers. "Wait a minute. I think that was the guy somebody took out a few days ago. It was in the papers. Name like that sticks with you."

"I don't think so," Ralph said. "Gotta be somebody else." He took a good pull of his Sam Adams.

"Yeah," Mary Mike said, "this Russian—he was into narcotics, prostitution, money laundering, you name it. All across the board. And you can bet he was connected, Ralphie, if it's the same guy. He was one of the bosses, they said."

"He was whacked?" Ralph said. "No shit. Well, looks like somebody wants to whack him again."

Chapter 4

Fake News

A Few Minutes Later

Millie finished her beer. Cracked open another one. "So we're supposed to whack a dead guy?" Millie said. "Oh, boy, we'll need to advertise a special rate for that kind of job." A little irony for Ralphie.

"Should we charge more or less?" Ralph said.

Millie slid her eyes over at him. Is he being ironic too? I hope so. His expression was totally blank. No way to tell what he was thinking.

"I'll be right back," Mary Mike said. She left the room, returned a moment later with *The Boston Globe* article on the murder of Yuri Kuznetsov.

"Here it is, just like I said. Some of it's missing because I tore out a recipe for Irish soda bread from the other side. But you can see that the Russian guy's dead. Somebody whacked him last week, so how can Philly have a contract on him?"

She handed the ripped page to Millie. Mary Mike was right:

Jerry Masinton

RUSSIAN MOB CHIEF SLAIN

By Wallace Mainwaring

    Yuri Kuznetsov, believed to be a member
of the local Russian Mafia, was gunned
down yesterday outside his home in
Brookline. The killing was gang-related, say the police. No suspects have
been identified.

    This morning, Boston Russian Radio
reported that two listeners calle claiming the murder was "fake," a plot by
Federal agents to protect Mr. Kuznetzov
who agreed to turn state's evidence in
the upcoming conspiracy trial of two

The rest of the article was missing. Maybe it was in Mary Mike's recipe book, Millie thought, sticky with bread dough. Interesting development, though.

"OK, he's either dead or not dead," Millie said. "Who are they going to bury if Yuri is in some motel room throwing down Smirnoff shots with the Feds?"

She offered the torn sheet to Ralph. "Nah, I don't read the papers," he said. "You can't trust 'em. The sports, yeah, they're OK. The politics, uh-uh, it gives me a headache. Remember when you iced Joey Di Marco's guys in Des Moynes, Mil? Mary Mike here showed me the paper. Terrorists, they said, blowin' up the country. It's all fake news."

"D'Angeli, Ralphie. His name was D'Angeli, remember? We're lucky the papers got it wrong. So did the police. The papers just reported what the police thought was true."

They had cleaned the table and put the dishes into the dishwasher. Millie was sipping her Sam Adams. Ralph and Mary Mike were making steady progress with the Jack Daniel's Black.

26

"So whaddya think? How we gonna accept a contract on a dead guy who could be in custody somewhere?" Ralph said. "On the other hand, we maybe contact the client, jack up the price, and say, 'Look, we take a look, but we got nothing to go on yet, but if we find your guy we'll do him. Plus, half the money's got to be paid up front. Otherwise, we got no deal.'" He drained the rest of his Jack Black.

"Don't do that yet, Ralphie," Millie said. "Philly said this is a hurry-up job, right? I don't like to be rushed."

"Yeah, that's what he said, the client's in a hurry."

"How are we supposed to hurry things up," Mary Mike said, "if we're in the dark here and have to go out looking for this Russian? It could take time. I think we take a pass on this one, Ralphie. Millie, dear? You're the shooter." She pulled her hair loose, shook it, started to braid it.

Millie turned to admire Ralph's money tree in the next room.

"We should probably take a pass, yeah," she said.

"Ralphie," Mary Mike said, "we just tell Philly what we know, which is nothing. If Kuznetsov is actually dead, which I'm voting yes he is, otherwise why would *the Globe* say so? That's not enough for us to get involved."

"I told you, you can't trust the fuckin' papers. Include the TV there too."

"Ralphie, dear, think a minute," she said. "*The Globe* is a respected newspaper, right? They can't afford to print information that people can check if it's wrong." She reached for her glass, held it up to eye level for inspection.

"You have a pal who's a reporter for the *Globe*, Ralphie," Millie said. "The guy you went to high school with. Ask him. You used to date him, didn't you?" Millie riding an old joke.

He just looked at her. "Him and me talk sports, sometimes, when I see him at Dippin' Donuts. I can't ask him about this. He'll say why do I want to know and then what do I say? 'Oh, you know, I heard you had a story about this dead Russian who's gonna testify in court, that's all.' Then he'll say, 'I thought you didn't pay attention to the papers, Ralph, just Ryan and Shaughnessy for the sports.' He knows I'm not interested in crime."

"He won't be suspicious, Ralphie," Millie said. "You're just making conversation."

"Just a minute, let's think about this for a second," Mary Mike said. "OK: The government, the police, whoever—it looks like they were in bed with this Russian gangster to—to what?—testify against some other gangsters? That's what the paper said. Then somebody took out the guy before he could testify."

"Mary Mike's right, Ralphie" Millie said. "Pretty hard to fake this."

"Yeah, OK, it makes sense," Ralphie said. "I'll tell Philly we're out."

"Here's another thing," Millie said. "Why would these people call the Russian radio station and say the guy's murder was staged? One call I can believe. But two? There's a fishy smell."

"Why can't we just have a simple whack job anymore?" Ralphie said. "Used to be, you get a phone call, couple of days later you get the guy's photo or where he works, maybe who he's banging, you know, and then you take him out, bing bing bing. Nothing to it. Now, you get . . ."

"What the hell do you fucking mean, Ralphie— 'nothing to it'?" Millie said. "How many guys have you iced? Jesus Christ, bing bing bing. This isn't a video game you're playing with some fat guy on his couch in Cleveland where you have pee breaks and eat Snickers. Where's your head?"

"No, I didn't mean it like that, Mil, I just meant I

don't like it when the target's already dead, see?"

"Well, it'd be easy money. You could even do it yourself."

The room was getting darker. Clouds building up outside. Millie switched on the lights over the kitchen counters. Very cozy, she thought. She took a tumbler from the cabinet and brought it to the table.

Mary Mike poured her some Jack, fattened up Ralph's glass and her own. She said, "That's that, then, we tell Philly we don't shoot corpses and to relay our decision back to the client. We're out."

"Yeah," Millie said. She sipped her drink. "But I'm thinking what if this Yuri is really alive and the Feds or somebody 's pulling a fast one, like the radio said? Who's the dead guy, then? And who the hell is the client?" She downed the rest of her drink, set her glass gently on the table. "Mostly, why contact us? That bothers me. Listen, Ralphie, call our guy in Philly. Ask him if he can track down the client. I'm just curious."

"Don't even think about it, dear," Mary Mike said. "You said so yourself. We don't need this kind of trouble. Give me your glass. So what you're saying—we should reconsider?"

"Let's just find out who's paying for the hit. Maybe the guy hasn't read the papers yet."

"What the hell do we care who the client is, if we're not in?" said Ralph. He looked tired, Millie thought. He's done a lot of talking today. And don't forget the bourbon.

"I'm not saying we commit. Let's check out the players on the board—on the off-chance something's out there that we don't like. It's my Army training."

"Yeah, but you know what my mother used to say, Mil?" Ralph said.

"Please, not your mother again, Ralphie," she said. "How many times . . .?"

"She told me, 'Ralphie, what you don't know won't hurt you,'" he said. "She musta told me that a hunnerd times."

"Maybe you were a slow learner."

"I was just making conversation, Mil. Mary Mike's right: The job feels wrong."

"Sure, that's why we've gotta ask some questions."

"Like what?" Mary Mike said. She was on her fourth or fifth hit, Millie guessed. Hard to keep track. Ralph was trying to keep up with her.

"Just what I said: Start with the client, M—find out who he is," Millie said. "We don't want to spend our time hunting down corpses for some lunatic."

"OK, we can try that," Mary Mike said. "What else?"

"A recent photo of Yuri, preferably while he was still breathing."

"Philly's probably already on it," Mary Mike said. "Part of the routine."

"One other thing, M. Find out if there's going to be a funeral for our Russian friend. Who knows—maybe he'll be there in a casket with fresh makeup and a nice smile for us."

"Millie, dear, you're not planning to go to his funeral, are you?" Mary Mike said. "The place will be filled with Russian gangsters."

Her braids had come loose. Her hair was reaching the Phyllis Diller stage.

"And then what if it's closed casket?" Mary Mike continued. "It could be Jimmy Hoffa in there, for all we know. And what if they start asking questions?"

"I'll tell them I don't speak English," Millie said.

Chapter 5

What We Talk about When We Talk about Movies

Tuesday Evening

Millie and her partner Mandy were in bed watching a Bogart movie, *In A Lonely Place*. Their backs resting against the padded headboard, eating Orville Redenbacher's Movie Theater popcorn. Their après sex soul food. Mandy was wearing her Minnie Mouse pajamas, Millie a black T-shirt and drawstring bottoms.

Mandy—Amanda Press Bradford—was descended from William Bradford, the second governor of Plymouth Colony, who had sailed on the *Mayflower* to the New World for religious freedom. The ship was supposed to land in Virginia, but ended up at Cape Cod, which was OK with Mandy, who had little interest in either geography or family history. But she did enjoy her freedom to pose nude for *Punt: The Man's Man's Magazine*, which had a legally murky but highly profitable connection with Polly Rose Associates, a small talent agency run by Emerson Byles.

Amanda was just Priss to Millie, who also figured that the less you know about your ancestors the better off you are. In fact, though, she couldn't trace her ancestors back any farther than her grandmother on her mother's side.

Mandy's love-name for her was *"Tesoro"* or "Tes," meaning "treasure" or "darling" in Italian.

"So, Emerson says to me," Mandy said, "'Sweetheart, watch this film, see if you think Gloria Grahame's sexy in that really killer way. I'd like your special viewpoint, you've been to Yale and I admire your intelligence, and I'm just trying to decide how she burned through so many guys on and off the screen, OK?'

"Notice how he calls it a 'film,' Tes, like he reads *Cahiers du Cinema* instead of *Punt*," Mandy said, "and you should have heard the way he said 'Chweehard,' trying for that tough-guy Bogart growl, and you know Emerson, *Tesoro*, he was serious, he wasn't playing it for laughs."

"You forgot to press the Pause button, Priss," Millie said. "Now we have to go back a few minutes. We just finished that great scene in the detective's office when Grahame gives Bogart an alibi. I want to see it again."

"Shit, I'm sorry, Tes. We need more popcorn anyway. Back in a jif." She slid out of bed and did a little dance into the kitchen. Minnie Mouse with a bounce. What a perfect ass, Millie thought. Eat your heart out, Gloria Grahame.

Back in bed, Mandy said, "God, Tes, this is great popcorn. Oh, I forgot the napkins, our new comforter is going to be covered in butter."

"Here, use this." She reached over to her nightstand, handed Mandy an old khaki T-shirt from her Army days. "Needs to be washed anyway."

"Theng-kyou." Mandy wiped her mouth. "OK, let me just finish. Emerson's obsessed with Gloria Grahame, he can't stop talking about her. I said to him, 'Emerson, give it a rest, just let me see it and I'll give you the full-on lesbian file that you're dying for,' and he said something like, 'Wait a minute, Chweehard, I'm interested in your mind, not who you sleep with,' and here I am straddling a Harley with nothing on but boots and a micro-mini and my nipples turning blue in the air-conditioning, and I said, 'Emerson, for god's sake, Lorenzo'—that's our photographer—'Lorenzo is patiently trying to get a good angle on my crotch, which you apparently cannot remove your fucking eyes from, while you tell me you respect me because I'm smart? I love it. Just put *le film* in my Vuitton over there, would you Chweehard?'"

"You have a hard life, Priss, I've always said so," Millie said. "Shall we watch the rest of this movie, or not?"

"Just one more thing, OK, Tes?"

"OK, finish what you were saying so we can see if Bogart's a murderer."

"I went online to check out this movie," Mandy said. "Bogart wanted Lauren Bacall in the female lead, but her studio wouldn't release her or something, and Gloria Grahame ended up with the part. Fine. They make the movie. But there was high anxiety during the filming. Grahame and the director, who's her husband at this time, are having marital troubles and they end up separating before the movie's wrapped.   And get this, Tes: he decides to sleep in one of the sets they're using for filming, and the two of them promise to keep it secret— to preserve the noble calling of art, I suppose. But the tension keeps building, and Grahame, professional to the bone, channels all this emotion into one of her best performances."

"The agony and the ecstasy of movie-making, Priss, what can I say?"

"Tell me about it. And anyway, I forgot to mention that the director had a son by an earlier marriage, I think his name was Tony."

"Tony's the kid or the director?"

"You're being a smart-ass, Tes. Tony is the kid. His dad the director is Nicholas Ray, a big deal with the gals back in 1950. Couldn't keep it zipped up. Now listen: I'm getting back to why Gloria Grahame has this reputation for sexiness and that femme fatale thing that Emerson can't get his mind off of. Off. Not long after the movie—excuse me, the *feelm*—wraps, I think it's a year or so later, our girl sleeps with little Tony, who's thirteen at the time. She's twenty-seven."

"Stop right there, Priss, unless it's true love that's happening. I wasn't raised that way. Pass the popcorn."

"So here's the shocker: Nicky walks in on them in bed together in the couple's Malibu home. That's what he claims, anyway. Can you believe it? I can't decide whether that'd make a good movie scene or not. Anyway, for various reasons Gloria's career starts to slide downhill. But when little Tony gets to be twenty-three—and this is the true-love part—he and Gloria get married. Is that beautiful, or what? By this time she's long-divorced from Nicky and I think another temporary husband."

"Well, I should hope so, Priss. Look, Emerson doesn't need to know all this stuff. It'd just upset him. Just tell him that Gloria was a high-octane hottie who had a vigorous and varied sex life, which did not always bring her happiness."

"I'm going to tell him that those aggressive metal bras that she and Barbara Stanwyck used to wear looked like weapons."

"Metal?"

"No, I don't know, Tes, but remember those bullet bras that they used to wear in the 40s and 50s movies? They looked lethal."

"Yeah. Sweater girls. They never did a thing for me. I'd rather look at your tits without a bra than theirs with hard D-cups." She lifted Mandy's Minnie Mouse pajama top and kissed both breasts.

"Oh, my goodness, Tes, I love your girls too. You

don't need any pointy bras to be devastating either. You'd be sexy in a nun's outfit—one of those medieval gala things—a habit, it's called. It'd have to be designed by Tisci or Versace, of course, you don't want an off-the-rack habit. Or you could be wrapped in, let's see . . . "

"Whoa, stop there, Priss. Let me think. A nun's habit—that's good. I've been trying to decide what to wear to a funeral on Saturday. Something that won't call attention to itself. But also roomy enough to hide my gear."

"An outfit that won't draw attention to you? Where's this funeral taking place, Tes—in Sicily? Transylvania? Not that it's a bad fashion idea, per se, but not for a funeral."

"It's in a Russian Orthodox church. Nobody'll notice me."

"Nuh-unh. Who cares if they notice you? They're not going to know who you are in any case. If I were you, I'd go in dark slacks and one of those criminally chic Theory Oaklane silk trench coats. Black lace-up dress flats. And designer dark glasses: Tory Burch with tortoise-shell rims would be perfect here. And one of those roomy Rebecca Minkoff shoulder bags for your gun. And a scarf—Elizabetta. You'll kill them."

"Yeah, that's probably what I'll end up doing. Now can we get back to the movie?"

Chapter 6

Father Dmitry

Wednesday Morning

Millie had a lot of stuff to do before the funeral. For instance: locate the funeral parlor that was preparing the body and find out who's actually going to be in the coffin.

Mary Mike helped her by making a few calls. They were in Ralph's kitchen drinking coffee and eating thin slices of toasted Irish soda bread slathered with butter. Ralph was out on his morning donut run.

Mary Mike turned on the speakerphone. First guy she called, Malachy McDonnell, who worked for *The Boston Herald*, told her that the undertaker's identity was supposed to be a secret. But he'd ask a guy who wrote obits for the paper and played poker with one of Boston's Finest every Tuesday night when the cop's wife was with her writing group. Maybe come up with something. He put her on hold.

A minute or two later he was back on: "OK, here's the scoop, Mary Mike. The cop thinks the body is with a firm called Stepanov and Mirsky, in Milton, but he's not sure. I asked Pollard, our obit guy, why this is classified information. He said, 'I asked Foley the same thing'—this is the cop—'and Foley said to me, "You know what Russian nesting dolls are?"' And Pollard said, 'Yeah, I know what they are. So then what, these guys are smuggling little wooden dolls into the country? And Foley told me,' Pollard said, '"Everything these damned Russians do is hidden inside something else, that's why it's a secret."' I hope that helps, Mary Mike."

Millie held up the slice of bread she was eating. "Is this the recipe you tore out of the *Globe* when you read about Kuznetsov?"

"Um-hmm. Do you like it?" Mary Mike said.

"God, M, you missed your calling."

"Hon, you can bake bread and still have a career. I'll give you the recipe."

Next, Mary Mike got in touch with Steve Yukovich, a guy she once worked with to wash money in the Caymans who also raised money for local Slavic churches. She figured he'd at least know where the service was going to be held.

"Hey, Mary Mike, how you doin'?" he said. He had an upbeat, friendly voice.

"Steve," she said, "I need some information."

"OK, I'm doin' pretty good myself, thanks for askin'," he said.

"Sorry, Steve, I'm in kind of a hurry and forgot my manners."

"That's OK, kid. What do you need?"

"Well, it's complicated, but I'd like to know for sure where the funeral for a guy named Yuri Kuznetsov is going to be held. This guy's a Russian mobster, he's supposed to be dead, but there's some doubt that he actually is, but if he is dead, I need to know where the funeral service is going to be. He's Russian Orthodox."

"So, the usual deal, eh, nothing's straightforward? Funny thing you called, kid. I keep hearing rumors about the guy—Kuznetsov's his name, right?—that somebody posing as him got shot and that Kuznetsov is hiding out somewhere. But the *Globe* wrote it up that he got iced a few days ago, so I figure the rumors are bullshit. Did you read about that?"

"Yeah, I did. But why are there people out there who say the killing was faked?"

"And that's why you're calling me? I don't know. What difference does it make to you, anyway?"

"It doesn't. I'm making a scrapbook of Russian criminals, OK? It's a hobby."

"All right, all right, I get you. It's none of my business. Here's what I heard over to Saint Ambrose's, day or two ago. Not for publication."

"Steve, for god's sake . . . "

"OK, OK, never mind. There's a service on Saturday at Saint Nicholas there. Family and friends only. Officially no name given out for the deceased. Unofficially it's your guy. The rector is Father Dmitry Peskov. You'll have to confirm it with him."

"I don't know him, Steve. Why would he talk to me, especially if it's a big secret?" Pause. "Can you pave the way for me? You said it yourself, it's impossible to do anything straight-on when you're dealing with the Russians."

"It'll cost you, babe. But you probably already know that. I'll get back to you."

"Do you trust this guy Steve?" Millie asked Mary Mike. She helped herself to a third slice of the buttered soda bread. Filled Mary Mike's coffee mug and her own.

"Absolutely. If he needs something from me, I give it to him, no questions asked. When I'm doing the asking, it's the same for him. Complete trust."

"Like Girl Scouts, right?"

"Yes, I suppose so, dear."

The phone rang: Steve Yukovich.

"Father Dmitry said," Yukovich said, "he is *schastlivyy*—that means 'happy'—to help us, in strictest confidence, but you gotta understand that means a donation. For himself, he wants nothing, of course," Yukovich said, "but for God a new altar."

"I'll pony up two grand, Steve, but not a rubel more," Mary Mike said. "And remember, this phone call never happened."

"Hey, c'mon," he said. "Whadda ya take me for? Me and you go way back—back to Saint Luke's where we stole Sister Barbara's bag of candy that she wasn't supposed to eat during Lent. Remember that, kid?"

"I remember that we got our knuckles broke for our trouble, Stevie, and got sent home for a week. That was the last time I listened to you. Now what else do you have for me?"

"Good times, weren't they?" he said. "OK, Father Dmitry told me, he said, yeah, Stepanov and Mirsky are preparing your dead guy. In fact, S and M has a deal—here's how he put it—'to making *krasivaya* the past bodies of the faithful of Saint Nicholas.'"

"What does 'classy via' mean?"

"'*Krasivaya*,' kid, it means beautiful. These undertakers make the past bodies beautiful. Get it? Not a bad way to put it."

"OK, yeah, now give me the number of this priest so we can do business. And Stevie—I owe you one."

She called the rectory. Millie listening, taking it all in.

Father Dmitry was expecting Mary Mike's call, his secretary said, but he would have to be disturbed in his meditations. But was it urgent, she said, and if it was she would wake him up.

Yes, Mary Mike explained, it was urgent.

She waited almost five minutes to speak to Father Dmitry, who sounded jolly and eager when she mentioned the money. "For Mr. Yukovich I do this," Father Dmitry said, "and because you are good person."

"But you don't know me, Father," Mary Mike said.

"Yes, but you call church, and for this you are good person. And to donate for the new altar. Church of the Annunciation, they have new altar and want to steal my flock. Now you help me, so I say a special prayer for you. But two thousand, you understand? Maybe buys the altar cloth. My church is poor."

"OK, Father, how about five thousand, and you throw in a little extra incense. So now tell me, is the funeral ceremony for a man named Yuri Kuznetsov? We want to pay our respects. And we want to send flowers to the undertaker."

"Yes, is Kuznetzov. I have to do special for him because he was not believer. But God will accept him when I say prayers. You understand? You are Orthodox too?"

"My name is Mary Mulloy, Father."

"Ah, I see. Yes."

"And the undertaker, Father, who is that?"

"Is Shtepanoff ant Meershky," he said. "Is the best work. They make beautiful the dead people for God. And the low price too, because we give to them all our bodies guaranteed."

Mary Mike ended the call. "I knew I couldn't get anywhere with two grand," she told Millie. "Actually, I think we got off pretty good. But we still don't know any more than we did. You heard him, he said the funeral is for Kuznetsov. The guy's dead, like the papers said."

"So what has your five grand bought, if you're right?"

"At least we know where the funeral is."

"But Father Dmitry doesn't know who's going to be in the box, does he? He's just taking somebody else's word for it."

"Why are you so suspicious, dear?"

"Because I'm beginning to think there might be two guys out there claiming to be Kuznetsov. A live one and a dead one. And I'd bet that the contract isn't for the dead one."

Chapter 7

Anton Poliakov

Later Wednesday Morning

The large open room at the front of the funeral parlor looked like the one Millie had seen in her Aunt Rita's retirement home, though maybe a little cheesier: 1940s-style sofa, chairs, and curtains covered in the same flowered fabric. Brick fireplace with one of those Bulova mahogany mantel clocks like her Grandma Esther used to have. On the floor a light-blue rug that had seen its best days under President Harry Truman.

She walked to a small, tidy desk to her right and tapped the silver service bell. The bell sounded like a cricket. "Hello," she said. "Anybody here?" She tapped the bell a couple of times more. More crickets, but no echoing voices.

She tried another "hello" and got more silence. Time for a little recon. She remembered something Ralphie had said yesterday: Why can't we just have a simple hit? Somebody contacts us, we ice the guy, and then we collect. This fucking business with the church and now the funeral home was getting to be a major headache.

The large room at the left side of the entrance had bright new caskets on display. Burnished metal, gleaming mahogany, another kind of polished wood that she couldn't identify. All of the caskets had plump, pillowy satin linings. In the background, barely audible, she heard soft, depressingly sweet music. To remind the mourners of the dreariness that lay in wait for them?

Down the hall from the big front room were two offices with clean desks and artificial plants in the windows. No evidence that anyone worked in either of them.

At the end of the hall, a dark stairway. She followed it down to a dim basement with scuffed linoleum on the floor.

She walked past two cheap wood hollow-core doors with dents kicked in them, then came to a metal door with a small window. She looked in—the embalming room. On the near side of the room a long, gleaming steel table with drains along the edges, a large lamp hanging over it from the ceiling. Next to the table a metal cart with two shelves. On the top shelf, trays filled with knives. On the bottom shelf, a stack of folded white towels. Behind the embalming table, on a long counter, she saw a thin steel pole about a yard long. Jesus, a trocar. On the far side of the room there was a second table—this one with a body on it.

The body was covered with a clean white sheet. Sitting next to the table was a thin man in a white lab coat, fortyish, with wiry electrified hair—part Gene Wilder, part Albert Einstein. His heels were pumping up and down in time to the music being piped into his head by two white earbuds. His head was bobbing. Enjoying himself in this house of the dead. Getting psyched up before slicing into the body, she figured. He was facing away from the door.

Millie knocked. He didn't hear. She opened the door, inhaled stale air and the acrid stench of embalming fluid, walked over to the man, and tapped him on the shoulder.

He shot up from the folding metal chair, which fell over and clattered to the tiled floor. His earbuds fell out. "Dun shoot!" he said. "I am Poliakov!" He raised his hands high in the air. Fingers wagging.

"Why would I shoot you?" she said.

"I am not owner. I am Poliakov. I have green card."

"Put your hands down, Poliakov, OK?"

He lowered his hands, but his fingers seemed to be playing an invisible keyboard. "You are here why? In this room?"

"I have a question or two. Do you mind?" Wondering how the man could stand the odor in the room—not just the embalming fluid. Something rotten and something else she couldn't identify.

"You are police."

"I'm not a cop, Poliakov. I'm a paid assassin. You don't have to be afraid."

"You make joke. I understand. Amedican humor."

She showed him the Glock, then put it back into her bag.

"OK, I am wrong. Maybe I am not going to die."

"Just shut the hell up and talk to me. Be serious." She was glad she'd left the door open. Thin out the heavy smell of death.

"Yah, sure," he said, "now down to business, that's how you say it—down to business? But be fast, OK? I have big job to do. You dun wan be here when I work. Is against the law, too."

"Look, nobody was out front. The place looked like a morgue. Sorry. I meant the place seems empty except for you. I need to know something. Maybe you can help me."

"We do business, then, OK. That means money?"

"That means I don't shoot you and put you on the second table here."

"I am innocent man. I know nothing. Stepanov and Mirsky, they are the crooks. Sometimes they put two dead bodies in casket, I confess to you this in private. Sometimes they put stranger, if client requests. I am just—how you put it?—higher hand."

"Hired hand. What's your first name?" she asked.

"Is Anton. Where I come from Poliakov is big name. My great-grandfather own one hundred kilometers land square in Ukraine. Fucking Stalin take it from him." Anton spat on the floor. He picked up the chair that had tumbled backward. Sat down. Crossed his arms.

The fluorescent lights were making a soft, sizzling sound.

"OK, look, Anton, whose body are you preparing for the funeral this Saturday at Saint—I can't remember—Father Dmitry's church? Saint Nicholas. Could be worth a few bucks after all."

"Yes, is big secret, they tell me. Why, I ask? Dead is dead. How much you pay?"

"Depends on your answer. So tell me. Who's on the slab there? Is it a guy named Kuznetsov?"

"You know this name? How? Is all of a sudden popular guy."

"Just a good guess. Am I right?"

"Is maybe Kuznetsov. But maybe not. There is much talk, how to do this one, where to put him, who pays for him."

"Maybe Kuznetsov, maybe not—what the hell. Make up your mind, Anton, who is it?"

He stood up, agitated.

"Is not Kuznetsov, I think. Is another man. But we say Kuznetsov anyway. This I hear Mirsky say on the phone. He ask this person, 'You tell me this is Yuri Kuznetsov here, yes? OK. Fine. I dun want trouble.' And then Mirsky get excited and say, 'OK, OK, no problem. Is Yuri Kuznesov, I believe you. We have here papers. Sure, whatever you say, Boris.' So now I dun think he's Kuznetsov, maybe."

"When did you receive the body?"

"They dun tell me. Three days, four. What do I know? They put him in cooler. This morning I take him out. Soon I will prepare."

"What name did he have two days ago?'

"Mirsky make wrist band: 'Ivan Podolsky.' Then he make new one after phone call. He put on counter with papers, shake head, and leave—very fast. One hour ago."

"And that's this guy?"

"Yes, is Podolsky, I think, before he is called Kuznetsov."

"So you don't really know Kuznetsov?"

"No, is stranger to me."

"What if you saw a photo?" She checked her iPhone. Mary Mike hadn't yet forwarded any pics from Philly.

"Who knows? Is maybe possible."

"Lift the sheet," she said. "I want to see what this guy looks like."

Poliakov folded back the sheet. The skin of the dead man was light blue and gray, wrinkling here and there. Purple lips and dark, sunken eyes. Dark thick hair combed straight back, dry-looking. Lips pulled back in a tight grimace. An odor like freezer burn and a hint of rotting eggs.

Millie got up close, bent over the corpse, looked at the wrist band: PODOLSKY, IVAN//CREMATE? She took a few snaps with her iPhone.

"So then this is Podolsky. Where are the new documents?"

"I have here." He picked up a manila file from the counter behind the table. "Mirsky put here, just before phone call. I don't read it yet." He handed it to her. Inside: a death certificate for Kuznetsov, Yuri. Signed by R. Vasilevsky, M.D.

She showed it to Anton. He nodded. "Good thing we check. But now we have big fucking problem." With his left hand he pulled his wiry hair. Then he closed his eyes and nodded his head several times. Agreeing with thoughts he'd rather not have, she figured.

"Somehow I'm not surprised, Anton, but why don't you let me in on the secret."

"OK. Is not Kuznetsov, this man." He back-handed the chilled-out guy on the table.

"We already know that," she said. "So where's Kuznetsov?"

"Who knows? Maybe we cremate him by accident. And now Mirsky, he gives me here this wrong body. This fucking Podolsky is an impostor."

Chapter 8

Call Me Popov

Wednesday, 5:00 p.m.

So why'd he say that this guy Podolsky was an impostor?" Ralph said. "Ain't Podolsky Podolsky?"

They were in Ralph's kitchen, eating take-out from Le Du Thai Eatery on Walnut Street. Ralph's treat. It was sunny and still warm outdoors. Millie felt good—calm, relaxed, cruising on automatic.

"You'd think so, wouldn't you?" she said. "But in this case Podolsky's not Podolsky. He's Popov."

"That was his alias?" Ralph said. He stirred the food around on his plate. Put his fork down. Then had a good strong pull of the Sam Adams in his mug.

"No. He had nothing to do with it."

"Sweetie, I might have missed something here," Mary Mike said. "There's a step in the middle I didn't see." She helped herself to more Pad Thai.

"The guy's real name was Popov. Or maybe not: It was the name in the record book for the guy the funeral home wrote up as Podolsky. It could have been any-thing."

"Well, dear, I'm not really sure that that clears it up for me. When you say 'anything,' I feel the way I used to when I danced the waltz with a fella named Daley. That was long before your time, of course."

"Meaning what, M?" Millie said.

"Meaning I'm not on solid ground when you say Popov, or whoever it was, that was in the mortuary records as Podolsky but could have been somebody else. How could they screw up the name? And why?"

"OK, this is what I came away with, after getting Poliakov to come down off the fucking ceiling and tell me what he knew. Think of the whole funeral operation as a big scam—at least in the past couple of months, when unidentified bodies have been coming through the basement door and given made-up names—maybe by Mirsky, maybe by the guys who delivered the bodies, maybe by this Boris, whoever he is. The other partner—Stepanov—wasn't around. He spends most of his time now in Miami, apparently. Mirsky's running the business."

"OK, I got it," Ralph said. "Dead guys get fake names when they're brought in to the funeral parlor. That means somebody's being paid off."

"Umm-hmm. The people delivering the corpses didn't care what they were called. 'Bela Lugosi' or 'Boris Karloff' would've been fine with them. They just wanted to make the bodies go away."

"And what better way than to cremate them or bury them in a casket, all nice and proper?" Mary Mike said.

"Yeah, that's it. Ralphie, can you please pass the Pad Thai? It's off the charts today." Millie took a sip of her green tea. Looked at his plate. "You're not eating yours. Something wrong?" she asked.

"I don't know, I'm more of a pizza and burger guy, I guess, like you always said."

"So why'd you order this stuff?"

"Well, you know, Mary Mike here said . . ."

"I said you ought to try something new once in a

while, Ralphie, it won't kill you. You need to get out of your comfort zone, have an adventure for a change."

"Yeah, next time maybe." He pushed his plate away. "What about your guy Poliakov—have I got his name right, Mil? What was his part in this game?"

"He's innocent, practically a bystander. He works part-time for S and M. He's also paranoid by nature. He actually thought I was there to whack him. Can you believe that?"

"I can't imagine," said Mary Mike.

"Yeah. So he didn't want to see or know anything. When the corpses arrived, he'd fix 'em up for burial or whatever and ask no questions. There was never any trouble until a few weeks ago when Mirsky started to get mysterious phone calls after each delivery and Poliakov decided to look at the death certificates that Mirsky had to prepare. They were all phony."

"So he gets nervous, right?" Ralph said. "I don't blame him. He should of just got another job."

"Well, he does have another job. It's also part-time. He works at Star Market in the meat department. But I get your point, Ralphie. Anyway, he's past tense at S and M now. I told him to get the hell away from there. I actually told him he needs to disappear. Finish with Popov, drop out of sight, leave town."

"Disappear from everywhere?"

"Yeah. For a while."

"Sounds like he's got his ding-dong in the ringer," said Ralph. "But why's he in so much trouble for doing his job? He didn't know anything. He was innocent, you said." He drained the last of his beer.

"For doing an illegal job, Ralphie, and for being dumb enough to get set up as the fall guy by his sweetheart of a boss, Mirsky, who gave Anton the job of signing off on the bogus death certificates. By the way, Mirsky has now disappeared himself, with a bag full of dirty money. Russian Mafia money, if I had to guess."

"Do you get what the fuck's going on here, Mary Mike?" Ralph said.

"Just listen to the story, Hon', it's confusing enough as it is."

"The way I see it," Millie said, "Russian Mafia guys are executing other Russian guys—probably from another outfit—and recycling them through Stepanov and Mirsky."

"Recycling?" Ralph said.

"Giving them new identities for burial. That way there's no official record of who's actually dead. There's no way to trace them. And there's no evidence against the hitters."

"Yeah, but what about the phony names? You say they were made up. Don't they go into some kinda state records that can be double-checked?" Ralph said.

"I thought of that, Ralphie, but who's going to check on the accuracy of who's who among the dead if the funeral home submits the usual forms to the state?"

"The funeral director sends them in," Mary Mike said. "But somewhere along the line they have to match up with an individual's records already on file."

"Well, maybe that's why Mirsky ran away," Millie said. "Somebody doing a records check finds out that dead people who never existed are being prepared by Stepanov and Mirsky. The guy gets in touch with Mirsky, asks him what the fuck, and Mirsky sees that the party's over."

"That could be it," Ralph said. "He knew he couldn't get out of the scam."

"We're guessing here, but yeah, it makes sense. The Russians would come into it too, don't forget. Poliakov told me that a guy named Boris called Mirsky just before I got there. Boris insisted that Mirsky had to identify the corpse in the embalming room as Kuznetsov."

"Boris wanted Podolsky to be Kuznetsov," Ralph said.

"It wasn't Podolsky, it was Popov, remember?" Millie

said.

"Oh, yeah."

"Mirsky said OK, but he was scared. A few minutes later he left with his hair on fire. Maybe he decided to move to Miami with his partner Stepanov—or more likely to Bear Creek, Idaho, or Mexico City—someplace where he figured nobody'd ever find him."

"The phone call scared the shit out of him," Ralph said. "So now he's running from the Russians too, not just the bureaucrats."

"Yeah. But who do you think he'd fear more—the state examiners or the Russian Mafia?"

"But if he went to another town, or like you said another country, he should be OK, right?"

"Ralphie, how far do you think you'd have to go to feel safe from the Russians?"

"Mil, people disappear all the time. This Mirsky could just grow a beard and change his name and he's home free."

"Yeah, that'd work, Ralphie. The Russians would never guess that he'd change his name. Do you have any suggestions? How about 'Popov'?"

"All right, all right, shoot me. Mirsky's out of play now—that's what you're saying. And we still don't know a fucking thing about Kuznetsov."

"Sure we do. He's alive and well. Dead men don't make this much noise."

"OK, so how do we find him?"

"I'll talk to Poliakov again before he leaves."

"He said the guy was cremated, didn't he?"

"He said maybe. Let's see if he'll change his mind."

Chapter 9

After-Hours Business

Wednesday, 7:30 p.m.

On her way home from Ralph's house, Millie phoned Poliakov and told him to meet her at the funeral home at eight o'clock. Street-level entrance at the back, where the stiffs were admitted.

He hadn't liked the idea of a meeting then—it would be dark.

"We already talk, I think. I have no more purposes for you. Now I am running away, like you say. I buy airplane ticket to Great Salt Lake City for my health."

"Odd choice, Anton."

"Yes, but is cheap ticket, so I clean shave and become Amedican citizen with the Moormens."

"The Mormons, are you kidding me? There are no foreign accents in Utah. Go to New York if you want to blend in."

"Yah, maybe. Maybe I try Tchicago."

"Listen, Anton, I need more information from you. Meet me in the prep room. Eight o'clock, not eight-oh-five, got it?"

"Now I see why you steal my phone number, so you can call me for dangerous assignment. I am dead man, right? You are part of plot to kill poor Poliakov."

"I could have iced you earlier today if I'd wanted to. Why bother with a damned plot?"

"Is the way I think. I am Russian."

At seven-thirty, Millie pulled into the parking lot at the back of the Stepanov and Mirsky Funeral Home. She turned off the headlights of her new midnight black Camaro. The tires crunched quietly over the gravel as she drove to the double doors on the basement level. The only light was a tiny bulb glowing above the double doors. Deep shadows everywhere. Overcast skies.

There were no other cars in the lot. She backed the Camaro into a dark space at the side of the building. The lot would appear empty to anyone looking at it from the street. The big-bore engine purring like a puma.

Her Glock was holstered over her right hip. She carried two extra mags in a pouch clipped to her jeans on the left side. She also had her Sig Sauer tucked into an under-dash pistol carrier with a custom quick release invented by Mr. Moustakas, the firm's clean-up man and weapons specialist.

Millie killed the engine and waited. She could see the double doors from where she sat in the shadows. She visualized the hallway leading to the prep room, the room itself, the two tables, the counters, the four-body refrigerator in the corner. Trying to remember every detail, every angle, every half-hidden corner. Thinking about shooting angles. While she was doing this, she saw the doors open.

A man stepped out on to the concrete apron and braced the doors open. He returned to the building. A moment later he returned, pushing a gurney. Light reflected dimly off its metal top and sides. The man looked around.

Poliakov.

A car entered the parking lot from the alley. Black Chrysler 300. Big back seat, big trunk. The Chrysler got about ten feet from the open doors and stopped, its headlights shining directly at Poliakov and into the building.

The driver and passenger got out, leaving the headlights on. Big burly men, both wearing long black-leather jackets, tight T-shirts. They had thick, swept-back hair. One of them had a big mustache. Like that old football coach with the big square head, she thought. Dudek? No—Ditka. Always wearing a scowl.

The men approached Poliakov. The driver, using his right index finger, poked him in the chest. Poliakov shook his head, shrugged his shoulders, lifted his hands palm out. The driver walked to the back of the car. Opened the trunk.

Poliakov followed with the gurney. He and the passenger lifted a dark shape out of the trunk and flopped it on to the gurney, then rolled the gurney on to the concrete apron in front of the mortuary doors. An after-hours customer for S and M, Millie thought. No wonder Mirsky skipped out. Looks like the Russian Mob has taken over this operation.

Poliakov half-turned and said something to the driver. The guy back-handed him and he staggered to the side. He regained his balance and the three entered the building.

These guys are going to force Anton to fill out phony paperwork for the corpse, Millie figured, and who knows what else? They'll make the usual threats and ask the usual tough-guy questions.

Will they squeeze anything out of him about me during the Q and A?

You should have just said no, and no again, she thought, to this fucking deal at the beginning, instead of following your curiosity all the way to a run-down funeral home at night watching a couple of assholes out of a bad B-movie with a corpse they need to unload.

If Anton says anything the least bit funky in there, those bozos are going to be waiting for me. How far will they push him?

She slipped out of the car. Eased the door shut. Walked to the double doors, hugging the building all the way, staying in the shadows. She held the Glock with both hands, police style, keeping it pointed up. The silencer was screwed on. On her hands, tight black leather gloves.

The headlights of the Chrysler pointed down the long hall leading to the prep room. Millie moved to the open doors, glanced in, and saw nothing but the brightly lit hallway. There was no sound.

She couldn't wait where she was because she was directly in front of the headlights herself and would be seen by anybody driving into the lot. Not to mention the thugs with Anton.

For a brief moment she thought of turning off the car lights and sneaking down the hallway in the dark. But no: If Anton has opened his mouth, they'll just be waiting to ambush me.

She decided to leave the lights of the Chrysler on, open the driver's door, and crouch behind it. I'll wait till they make a move, she thought.

She looked at her watch. 7:50. How long do I wait?

The two goons appeared a few minutes later, without Poliakov. They didn't seem to be in a hurry. Neither man held a gun.

Millie stood up, half in the shadows, arms extended, the Glock's snout moving slowly from one man to the other. "Where's Poliakov?" she said. Took a step to her left so they could see the pistol.

The guy with the mustache started to reach inside his jacket but changed his mind when Millie squeezed off a couple of rounds at his feet. The other guy hadn't moved. He looked bored.

"I said, 'Where's Poliakov?'" Her voice was level.

"This Poliakov," the mustache said, "he is friend of yours? We don't see him." He brushed back his hair with his left hand.

At that moment, with surprising speed, the other guy rushed her, his head lowered. Millie got off two shots before he could get to her, the slugs entering his forehead. Then she rotated the Glock a few degrees to her left and shot the mustache as he drew a pistol from his waist band. Put another round into him when he seemed reluctant to fall down.

She walked to the mustache, turned him over, made sure he was dead. The other guy, she knew, was gone before he'd hit the ground. The pistol that the mustache drew was a Makarov, used by Russian soldiers, she remembered. She popped the magazine, pulled the slide back, ejecting the round in the barrel. Tucked the pistol into her back waist band.

The other guy also had a Makarov. It was in his jacket pocket, along with a silencer.

She screwed the silencer onto his Makarov, shot holes in each of the tires, and put a couple of rounds through the windshield. Then turned off the Chrysler's engine and headlights, popped the pistol's magazine, and ejected the round in the barrel. She kept that weapon too.

Her watch said 7:55. She stepped into the shadows and waited five minutes. No police, no traffic along the street, no onlookers, nothing.

It was 8:00. Find Anton.

Chapter 10

Too Many Bodies

Wednesday, 8:00 p.m.

The prep room was lit up, but nobody was in it. On the counter at the back she saw two manila files with official-looking papers spilling out. Death certificates, she figured.

"Anton!" No reply. Did they take him upstairs and kill him? No, doesn't make sense. She tried again: "Anton!" The only sound was the hum of the refrigerator.

There was no blood on the floor. No signs of struggle. She picked up one of the death certificates. It was for somebody named Dobrynin, Alexander. Cause of death: "gunshot wound, base of skull." She picked up the other one: Bogdanov, Viktor. Cause of death: "gunshot wound, left temple." Both signed by R. Vasilevsky, M.D. Fakes. Mob killings, forged documents.

But where the hell is Anton?

OK, Millie, think. How would those bozos operate? First of all, where is the body they just delivered?

Of course: She turned to the four-body refrigerator in the corner.

She yanked open the door of the chest-high upper-left compartment. There was no body on the metal tray inside. She had better luck with the lower-left compart-ment. A white sheet had been carelessly tossed over a man. She lifted it to look. Blood-stained clothes, the blood not yet dark. The dead guy from the Chrysler. She got up close. Cause of death: gunshot wound, base of the skull. What a surprise. Powder burns indicate close range. The shooter signing off Mob-style.

She tried the upper-right door. Empty. What're the odds, Millie, that Anton's in the last one, and is he alive or dead? What was the name of that fucking cat that was both dead and alive?

She found Poliakov in the lower-right compartment. Dressed, but without a sheet to cover him. He was turn-ing an interesting shade of blue. His wrists had been taped to the sides of the tray. Tape covered his mouth. Duct tape. What would we do without it?

He opened his eyes. His hair was starting to look frizzy.

"You at least should have worn your lab coat," she said. "How long could you have lasted in there?" She slid the tray out. Removed the tape from his mouth, then his wrists.

"Depends," he said, "where they set the thermostat. Maybe not too long. But is not too bad yet—I spend two winters in Moscow. I don't worry. I know you are com-ing to rescue me." He was shivering. The fluorescent lights in the ceiling were sizzling. The room smelled of death and something like freezer burn.

"Is a lab coat in that drawer," he said. "Please?" He pointed. She helped him put it on. It didn't stop the shivering. He began to walk around the room, rubbing his hands over his upper arms.

"And what if I hadn't got here, Anton? Why didn't they kill you before they put you on ice? That's what they should have done."

"Yes?" he said. "Maybe to send message, you think?" His teeth were chattering. He could barely speak.

"Enlighten me. What would the message be?"

"'Here is freezing to death dumb shit Anton Poliakov, he ask too many questions.'"

"More Russian bullshit, you're saying." Millie looked around the room. "Before we leave, I want to see the records from the past few months. The ledger, books, whatever you call them."

"They ask also—those two that put me in freezer. I tell them I don't have. I say Mirsky take them when he runs away."

"And that's when they put you into the cooler."

"No, they have first something for me to do."

"And what was that?"

"To sign for our mortuary that this dead man is delivered here today by legal means."

"I saw the phony death certificates. One body's here, but where's the body for the second death certificate?"

"They deliver later tonight, they say."

"But you had to sign for it now."

"Yes, they make me sign both."

"Why did the driver back-hand you out there?"

"I tell him we have already too many bodies from him. Why so many, I say?"

"And he didn't like it." She was getting a headache from the buzzing fluorescent lights. From these fucking Russians, too.

"I dun think so, no. He say to me, 'Your fucking business to have too many bodies, *zhopa*.' Then he slap me."

"What does that mean—*zhopa*?"

"Means 'asshole.'"

"Did they have any more questions?"

"No, just to sign for the bodies they bring."

"What's the guy's name?"

"They tell me Korsakov, Rimsky. But I think is somebody else. They are making joke."

She nodded, almost in admiration. Why did you think there would be normal logic behind all this, Millie? These guys are fucking homicidal clowns.

"And the body in the cooler—is that Dobrynin?"

"Yes, is Dobrynin." Poliakov had stopped shaking, but his hands were tucked under his armpits for warmth. He was standing in front of Millie now. "Is time to go now, I think, before they come back. You are in danger too."

She held up her hand. "So, they tape you to the tray and slide you into the cooler. They tell you that they'll be back later tonight with another body. 'Just wait there for us, Anton, OK? We'll be right back.' But since you signed both death certificates, they don't actually need you anymore. Let you think about that as you freeze to death. Another Russian joke."

"Yes, I am in big trouble then. You don't need to explain. Now we go, please. This time they shoot us both. We must leave." He threw off the lab coat and started for the door.

"Wait a sec, Anton, I have an idea."

"I dun like to wait, OK? We go."

"They're not coming, Anton. They're dead."

"They die? You don't tell me this earlier. They have accident?"

"Yeah, somebody shot them."

"Yes, I see. The paid assassin. You are very good. But now we must run also from the politsiya. I am begging."

"One more thing, Anton."

"You are torturing my nerves."

"We'll be quick. Follow me outside. Bring the gurney."

Chapter 11

A Harvard Education and a Yale Degree

Wednesday, 10:30 p.m.

Millie and Mandy were eating half-cheese, half-pep-peroni pizza from the joint across the street, Lenzini's Pizzeria. They were drinking a medium-bodied Shiraz bottled by Aldi that cost $7. Millie ordinarily wasn't a wine person, but with pizza what else are you going to drink? Well, you could drink beer, of course. Coke. Anyway, she'd had a good belt of Buffalo Trace in the shower after she got home. She'd stood in the shower until her skin was all-over rosy-warm and the stink of the mortuary was gone.

They were sitting on stools at the granite-topped counter that separated the kitchen area from the living room. Five-bulb light fixtures above them hanging from the ceiling. The apartment quiet, fragrant with the smell of baked cheese and pepperoni. Perfect, thought Millie. And also there was Mandy—beautiful, sexy, sassy: beyond perfect.

61

"I used your shampoo, Priss," Millie said. "Left my hair really soft. Nice aroma too. What's it called?"

"Funny, Tes, I don't remember offering."

"Woman warrior, Priss, returning from battle, needing a little pampering. Use your powers of empathy."

"You could have asked." She pursed her lips, softly kissed the air.

"Well, how about it?" Millie took a big bite of pizza. The work at S and M hadn't spoiled her appetite.

"Darling, everything I have is yours. You know that. It's called Alterna Ten, and it's hideously expensive, and I had to fuck half the men in the agency to afford it."

"Which means that you fucked either your boss Emerson or the latest intern-of-the-month. Which means that you ordered it from Amazon for a discount."

"Not Amazon, *Tesoro*, but an outfit that of all people Emerson uses for his rinse. Place called Arganics. Check it out. A few days ago I asked him if he uses a rinse to keep out the gray. I was just joking. Then I thought he might take umbrage, as we Ivy Leaguers like to say. But ... "

"Do we need the class snobbery, Priss? Pass the pepper flakes."

"But he didn't. He was happy, in fact, to tell me about this store." She handed Millie the shaker with the pepper flakes. Offered another slice of pizza, which Millie accepted.

"Turns out, Emerson wanted to talk about himself. Gaaa! I should have known better. OK, then he said, 'One day I caught a glimpse of myself in the mirror in the men's room, I'm sure you're familiar with those high unforgiving windows, and I could see the unmistakable signs of a cheap hair rinse.'"

"He actually said that?"

"'Why the fuck,' I said to him, 'would I be familiar with the windows in the men's john?'

"'Oh,' he said, 'figure of speech, darling, I don't mean

you do business in there.' Then he said, 'I could scarcely believe my eyes—the bluish drugstore tint.' And—get this—he actually pats his hair like, I don't know, George Clooney in that dumb movie when he wears a hairnet."

"Are we getting to the end, Priss? I've had a hard day at the office."

"Sure, almost done."

"Why didn't you just walk away, Priss? Tell him to piss off? That's always a good exit line."

"I know, I know, totally my fault. He was wound up, and I hadn't practiced my bitch-from-hell routine that morning. 'It looked like I bought it at Dollar General,' he said, 'even Alain saw it. But—and here I drew the proverbial line—he claimed that it had to be caused by a "follicular abnormality"—Alain's wretched term, not mine. You remember Alain,' Emerson said, 'my hairdresser who bleeds me white with every appointment?'"

"You should have told him you were having your period," Millie said, "and needed to rush out and buy a tampon."

"Of course, but I wasn't thinking. I thought he probably wasn't being serious, though with Emerson who knows? He's sometimes all flitty and jokey—either that or he's all Heathcliff and tragic. Then he asked me, 'Amanda, can you see it, darling, the blue trailer-trash tint in my hair? I want the truth.' He never calls me Amanda, Tes. I thought, he was edging toward desperate or possibly putting me on. I concluded he was fucking with me. I was in a hurry. So I told him, yeah, his hair looked like somebody'd painted it with Shinola. Suffice it to say, that wasn't the right answer. He took the aforementioned umbrage. But that's not all he . . ."

"You do have a stressful life, Priss. Don't you know that when somebody asks you to tell the truth about their appearance they're begging you to lie?" She had finished the last slice of pizza.

Mandy poured another glass of wine for herself.

Held the bottle up, tipped it toward Millie, and raised her eyebrows. Millie shook her head no. "This is shockingly good Shiraz, Chweehard," Mandy said. "How much did you pay for it? Did you have to fuck anybody?"

"Seven bucks," she said. "Aldi Shiraz. No, don't raise your eyes that way, Priss. The wine-shop guy told me that it beat out a $375 wine in some Australian competition. Who am I to question him? So—big spender here—I bought four bottles. Glad you like it."

"Well, aren't you a sly vixen?   So, to make a long story short, Emerson …"

"You're making a short story long. I'm almost down for the count. But go ahead."

"OK, then, bottom line: I order the Alterna Ten, which is no better than the Pantene that you and I share. Correction: that I buy and you share."

"Don't forget that I buy the pizza," Millie said.

"Sometimes."

"And bring home the bacon."

"'Bring home the bacon,' Mandy said. "Oh, there's a nice wholesome working-class expression. Much better than stuffy old 'take umbrage.' You know, Tes, Yale doesn't do nearly enough to teach its undergrads the right clichés. I'll have to talk to somebody about that."

"Talk to your dad. Isn't he on the board of governors or something?"

"Oh, yes, Daddy, he'd love to hear me on that subject. And while I'm on it, I could tell him that I take off my clothes for a living. Although some days I wear pasties if it's cold in the studio. He'd love that too."

"He's proud of you, Priss. Your prowess with the books, and all."

"Did they teach you that word at school, darling—'prowess'? Maybe the public schools aren't failing after all."

"Well, you know," Millie said, "government handouts to the underclass, the people who are too lazy to work for a living and send their kids to Groton or Brearley to prep."

"God, yes, tell me about it. Have you been visiting with Daddy?"

"He's a dear man. I'm sure he agrees with me."

"*Tesoro*, I have a question. OK?"

"Shoot."

"Really, sweetie, after today you might want to use another metaphor."

"I'm not myself, I guess. What's the question?"

"I've noticed something: Why do you like to play down your education? I mean it's like you want to hide the fact that you graduated magna cum from Harvard. And you're way smarter than me. Why hide your light under a basket?" She paused. "Ohmigod, Tes, I uttered a real-life home-spun cliché! It's your influence, sweetie, I just know it."

"I'll try to be more witty. Do comic impersonations."

"And something else I've been meaning to ask you," Mandy said: "Why did you get into the removals business? I've always wondered."

"Priss, I'm really tired. Besides, we've been through all that."

"Yeah, but you never really explain anything."

"Let's just say I wanted to give something back."

"Aw, that's sweet. But you worked your way through Harvard. You could be making a killing. Oops! I mean, a lot of money."

"You forget: I am making a lot of money."

"I feel like such a fucking failure, Tes. Daddy always paid for everything."

"He's not paying now. You're supporting yourself. You're putting your gold-plated education to good use, Priss. Think of it that way. You're bringing joy to millions—well, hundreds—of drooling, horny men who buy *Punt* to see your . . ."

"Yes, my fucking endowments, which only you can

ever actually possess."

"That gives me an idea, Priss. It's getting late. We'll clean up tomorrow. Let's brush our teeth, put on our p.j.'s, and see what happens."

"I know what's going to happen. You'll want me to rub your back. But it's my turn."

"I've had a rough day at the shop. My back hurts."

"A whiny assassin? Oh, please. What's wrong with your back?"

"I sprained it lifting those two bodies into the cooler."

Chapter 12

The Message

Thursday, 10:30 a.m.

Y ou stuck the fuckin' bodies in the freezer?" Ralph said. "What the hell for? You shoulda just got out of there. You weren't planning to—whadda ya call it—disembroil 'em, were you?"

They were in Ralph's kitchen. Two boxes of Dippin' Donuts, compliments of Millie Henshawe and Mandy Bradford, on the counter next to the fridge. Plus Dippin's coffee brewed from the store's own brand of beans. A bright, sunny day in Boston.

"No," Millie said, "though it's a thriving business there at Stepanov and Mirsky. It's 'disembowel,' by the way." She sipped her coffee. Closed her eyes with pleasure. I never get tired of this, she thought.

"Yeah, OK. I know you weren't gonna cut 'em open, but why waste the time putting 'em on ice? Why do you want all that extra exposure?"

"It just took a few minutes, Ralphie, and I wanted to send a message."

"Yeah? Like what? What did it say? Like that one in the movie—'Luca sleeps with the fishes'? Jesus, I liked that. Sorry, Mil, but I didn't think a woman could come up with something like that."

Mary Mike set her cup down on the table with perhaps more force than absolutely required by the laws of physics. "You'd be surprised, Ralphie, what women can come up with," she said. "Remember it was your ma and me that put Continental Removals together and gave it its reputation."

"Yeah, only Jesus, nobody's gonna think a woman—right? I'm not sayin' they couldn't—just that this is fuckin' smart."

"I wish your ma was here now, Ralphie, she'd say to you, 'Ralphie, women can do anything men can do, and probably better. Ginger Rogers danced as good as Fred Astaire, you know,' she'd say, 'and she had to move backwards—in heels, too.' Very few men can pull off what me and Sheila did. And don't you forget it. Here's your coffee."

"Me? No, I won't forget." He took a drink of his coffee. "That reminds me, about Dippin' Donuts. My pal Stuart there that has the franchise on Washington Street, he told me something yesterday. He said, 'Ralph, you won't believe this, but I gotta tell ya, the fuckin' guys at corporate, they went and changed the name of the business.'

"'What?' I tell him. 'What business? Yours?'"

"'Yeah,' he said. 'They sent down the word. This ain't Dippin' Donuts no more.'"

"You haven't read about this?" Millie said. "Everybody in town knows." She had four donuts on her plate—two old-fashioned and two Boston Kremes. She'd had a big workout earlier in the day.

"Where would I read it? You know I don't read the fuckin' papers."

"Oh, yeah, I forgot—'Ralphie don't read the fuckin' newspapers no more except for the fuckin' sports that Shaughnessy and that other one—Ryan's his name—

write for the *Globe*. Because, you know, for Ralph Klammer there, everything else is fake news.'" She topped up her coffee from the pot. It was almost empty.

"Jaysus, Millie, you sound like you just got off the boat from the Ould Sod," Mary Mike said. Playing along with Millie. "I never knew you could use the brogue."

"What the hell?" Ralph said. "What're you guys saying? What's she saying?" he asked Mary Mike.

"She's just having a little fun, Ralphie."

"But she never does that. Cut it out, Mil."

"Mandy told me I need to be more witty. I was just trying it out."

"Oh, yeah? Huh. I know you got a sense of humor, but sometimes I like it better when you talk normal, OK?"

"We'll see."

"Let me just finish my story here. Then we'll get back to business."

Mary Mike got up to brew another pot of coffee.

"So, OK, where was I?" Ralph said. "Oh, yeah: 'What's the new name?' I ask Stuart, 'because,' I said, 'why'd anybody want to change Dippin' Donuts to something else? That's gonna fool people.'"

"'Somebody at corporate,' he said, 'says we gotta be on the cutting edge—I don't know.'"

"'So what's the new name?' I said. 'Do I still come here to buy Dippin' Donuts, or do I go someplace else?'"

"'No, Ralph,' he said, 'you can't go no place else. That's the point. "Dippin'"—that's what we all gotta call it from now on. That's the new name. All the franchises.'"

"Ralphie," Millie said, "is this going to affect your whole life?"

Mary Mike went to the window, adjusted the shade to bring in more light. The whole scene reminded Millie of the re-runs of those old TV shows featuring the ideal American family enjoying time together in the kitchen.

She was aware of the irony.

"I just thought it was inneresting, that 'Dippin' is all we can say now."

"Ralphie," Millie said, "where the hell're we going here? We've been talking about Dippin' Donuts like we're the new franchise on Cabot Street, dressed up in our loony orange and brown costumes, making a commercial for morons."

"That time of the month?" Ralph said.

"That's good, Ralphie, real good," she said. "You're trying to be witty too. I'll have to tell Mandy." She picked up a chocolate glazed, dunked it, downed half of it in one bite. "No, I just think that we ought to talk about what we're going to do with the damned Russians. I've already put two of them out of business, not that I regret it, but I could come up with a lot of reasons why I shouldn't just go around shooting people."

"Yeah," Ralph said, "I wanna ask you something. After you stuck those two in the freezer, how'd they look?"

"What? They looked dead, Ralphie. What am I supposed to say—they looked like they were sleeping?" She helped herself to two regular glazed.

"OK, OK, I meant you didn't stop to clean 'em up, so they're gonna look suspicious, how they got there."

"No kidding." Not a question.

"Who's gonna identify 'em? Didn't you tell us that your pal Poliakov is leaving town soon and the owners are permanently on vacation?"

"Yeah, Anton's considering a change for his health. He decided after last night to go somewhere warm and sunny. Maybe Florida, where Stepanov is. But Mirsky? He's not on permanent vacation, Ralphie. He's permanently dead."

Mary Mike lifted her head. "How do you know?"

"I'm pretty sure. He left the mortuary in a big hurry, you remember, after talking to that guy Boris, who was giving him orders on handling one of the bodies coming in. Mirsky was scared shitless. And when he ran, he became a liability to Boris, because Mirsky knows where all the bodies are buried. Pardon me, Ralphie, that just slipped out."

"No, that's OK, Mil."

"So the Russians aren't going to let him get away. As for the two gangsters in the cooler, the cops will ID them, no problem. They probably have sheets a mile long. The local Russians are all going to know who they are too—part of the gang that's been doing business at S and M. Why do you care who IDs them, anyway?"

"I'm just thinking, we need more information on these guys, that's all," Ralph said. "We're trying to follow up on the first one, Kuznetsov, so we can decide if we want the contract on him. He's gotta be in there somewhere with all of these other fuckin' Russians."

"That's right, Ralphie, that's what we'd like to know. Where he belongs in the mix. Who is who. But we don't. So I think we should drop the whole thing. I made a mistake thinking we ought to look into it. We've got a rule—stay away from the Mob. Russian, Italian, Transylvanian."

"I haven't heard about that last one. Christ, here in Boston?"

"I just mean that we're no closer to Kuznetsov than we were when Philly called. That photo that Philly just sent doesn't help much. We still don't know where Kuznetsov is. The only thing we know for sure is that there's going to be a funeral on Saturday for somebody called Kuznetsov. I don't think it's him, by the way. I think he's still alive. But forget him, we already have plenty of good business coming our way."

"Like who?"

"Like the woman in Kansas City who's married to a hothead who likes to slap her around to stay in shape. He's broken a few bones that she was fond of. She came into some money, wants to invest it wisely."

"We ought to take that one, Ralphie," Mary Mike said. "Millie's already talked with her. Cokie, her name is, right?"

"Yeah," Millie said. "If anybody ever needed to get rid of a lowlife husband, it's Cokie. I've looked into it—should be an easy job. In one day, out the next. We'll have a happy customer who still has money left over for champagne every breakfast. She'll make a good reference."

"Yeah, but Philly has a feeling that the client that wants Kuznetzov dead is getting jumpy and might be willing to double our fee if we nail this one quick. Hard to turn down easy money, Mil."

"Jesus Christ, Ralphie! We've gone down this road before. It took us right over the edge of the cliff. Remember? I told you already, this one smells rotten. It's nuts."

"Whaddya mean?"

"We're being played—that's what I mean. It's a set-up of some kind. Nobody pays double for a guy that's supposed to be low on the food chain." She looked over at Mary Mike. "Did you ever trace back the identity of the client?"

"No, hon', I haven't, and I'm starting to wonder: Why would anyone bother to start an operation like this? The Russian gangs, they already have plenty of hitters. They can take down anybody they want. Why come to us? So I don't think it's the Russians. I think it's somebody watching from the shadows who wants us to hit the Russians. Doesn't make sense any other way."

"Except that these jokers specialize in complicated plots. But yeah, I agree with you."

"Back to the message you sent, Mil," Ralph said, "with those guys you froze to death."

"I shot them first, Ralphie, remember? And then we put them into the cooler."

"Yeah, but the message. You forgot to tell me what it

said. You were thinking about that fish in *The Godfather*, right?"

"I'm not answering that, Ralphie."

"OK, OK. But what did they look like in the freezer there? Just ordinary dead bodies?"

"Well, they had bullet holes in them, but other than that, yeah. I put their pistols on their chest, and I folded their hands over them."

"The tires of the car shot out, shell casings all over the lot—some from one of their guns, some from your Glock—and now the guys that went there to kill Poliakov by freezing him, they end up popsicles themselves with their fuckin' pistols on their chest. The way you do with flowers in a casket, right?" Ralphie, all in one breath.

"I wasn't thinking about the flowers."

"But it was a message, right?"

"Yeah."

"What did it say?"

"I didn't print out the words, Ralphie. I just figured that it was the right thing for the two guys to end up where they'd put Poliakov. When their Russian pals find out, they'll get the right message. They'll see those two guys on ice hugging their guns, and they'll probably think, 'Is the way we do business. Is Russian, maybe.' That's how they'll figure out the right message—it'll be the one they'd be sending if they had done the job themselves."

"Yeah?" Ralph said. He turned to Mary Mike. "Do you get all this?"

"It's not rocket science, Ralphie," she said. "Their boss will understand what happened in the parking lot and why they ended up in the freezer. It's obvious. But the boss won't know who did it. He'll think it's some other Russians."

"Yeah?"

"He might think he knows, but he'll be wrong. Because Millie is nowhere in the picture. Same with the police—it'll be a mystery to them too."

"But she's the one that whacked those two. She's in the fuckin' picture that I see."

"Sweetie, she doesn't exist, as far as they know. The whole thing looks Russian. It was a genius idea, Millie, making it look like their style of business. Your bullet casings will be found in the parking lot, but what does that tell anybody? Nothing. They'll think another outfit, probably, whacking the guys in the Chrysler. Shooting out the tires with the dead guys' own guns—definitely a Russian touch."

"Huh." Ralphie.

"It's past noon," Mary Mike said. "I'm getting down the bourbon."

"Just in time," Millie said.

"Mil," Ralph said, "what temperature did you set the cooler at?" One side of his mouth was lifted—half-smile, half question.

"I turned the thermostat down all the way," Millie said. "Minus ten Celsius. Poliakov usually keeps it higher."

"What's that in American?" Ralph said.

"Fourteen degrees Farenheit."

"Jesus Christ! They'll be hard as rocks. What did Poliakov say about it?"

"'Is good joke,' he said. 'Those two, they will appreciate.'"

The Boston Station

Thursday, 12:45 p. m.

They'd been sipping Jack Daniel's Black and eating salted nuts since noon, Millie chasing the bourbon with mugs of icy Sam Adams. Ralph had changed into his new short-sleeve guayabera shirt. It was burnt orange, with two wide black stripes of vertical pleating and four pockets. He was also sporting his mail-order Mexican huaraches, which squeaked when he walked. Mary Mike was wearing her belted blue cotton dress. Millie had on jeans and an oversize black T-shirt to cover her Glock.

Ralph's phone rang. "It's Barney," he said. He didn't stop to consult the stars this time before answering: "What's up, Barn?"

Mary Mike signaled Ralph: Put it on speaker.

"You watch the news?" Barney said. "The two Russian goons got taken out? You think it's fake?"

"No, it ain't fake, I got it from the horse's mouth, but that don't put us an inch closer to the guy we're suppose to whack."

"OK, then, you got any ideas, Ralph?" Barney said.

"Yeah, sure, we got some ideas, but they don't get us into the red zone."

"You guys," Mary Mike said, "can't seem to remember the rule about first names. So I'm going to just remind you that we're in the security business as much as anything, and then I have something to say."

Barney: "Yeah, sure, Auntie."

Ralph nodded.

"OK, listen," Mary Mike said. "Either we get hard information on this Russian job—who ordered it, whether the target is still alive, where he's at—or we pull the plug. Which right now I think we ought to do. It's simple. If it wasn't so complicated," she said, "with a couple of Russian Mob guys already put away and the main guy somewhere off the map, we don't know if it's a set-up or what, though to us it doesn't stand up."

"I don't have anything more on the guy—Kubersky or whatever—than I told you last time," Barney said. "I'm just getting nervous—one reason why I called, see if you and your guy there got anything fresh. And I don't think this is a business where you go in without all the aces."

"No," Ralph said. "I said we don't have zilch. So I guess we're all agreed, right?"

He looked at Millie. She nodded.

"Yeah," Barney said.

"And so then," Ralph said, "you tell the client, you tell him, 'Look, we can't get a lead on the guy you want to take down, and so therefore we can't put together a fuckin' operation, because nobody knows the fuckin' guy's whereabouts. We did our fuckin' best.'"

"Yeah," Barney said, "but I already relayed that message to the client, earlier today. I said, 'We're having trouble locating this guy because he's already dead, according to the cops, though we have our doubts.' And the client gets back pronto to Providence, who gets back to me, with: 'He's alive. Try the mortuary.' His exact words, according to Providence. So then I call you guys."

"The mortuary?" Millie said. "What the hell is that supposed to mean? I've seen all that S and M has on offer. There's no live or dead Kuznetsov there."

Barney: "Who's that on the phone? Your hitter that I've been hearing so much about?"

Ralph: "No, listen, Barn. You say Providence? Why didn't the Boston contact call you—isn't that the route?"

Barney: "That's the one that clipped those two Russians, isn't it? There at the funeral home? I'll be damned, talk about a fuckin' sweet job."

Mary Mike said, "Sweet merciful Jesus! Don't you know anything? I said security and I mean it! Stick to the subject. Now listen to me: Did you try to get back to the Boston station, see if the link was down?"

"Sorry, Auntie, I just got excited there," Barney said. "No, I didn't call Boston. I phoned Providence. I said, 'Why're you calling instead of Boston?' and Providence told me, 'Every time I tried Boston, it was busy or went dead, and then I had to try again. So, what the hell, I figured, I'll just call you instead.'"

"Has this happened before—did you ask him that?" Mary Mike said.

"Yeah, I asked," Barney said, and he said, 'Just today, after I sent out the message to the client that we can't hit a guy that nobody knows where he is.' Then," Barney said, "I told Providence, 'I'll pass it on to the boss.' Then I call you guys. So whadda ya think—run a check on the Boston line?"

"It might just be a little glitch," Mary Mike said. She closed her eyes for a second. "What was the other reason you called in? You said you had two."

Millie listening, taking it all in, yet a big part of her mind still thinking about "Try the mortuary." Why would the goddamned client mention the mortuary? How would he even know about it?

"Did I?" Barney said. "Oh, yeah—to see if you found anything new, and then this phone business. And while I'm at it, to say that this whole thing makes me nervous. I'm already jumpy, you know what I told Ralph, and then this fuckin' Russian contract comes along and throws me way off."

"You listen to me: There's no reason for you to be nervous," Mary Mike said, her voice gaining in altitude. "If we can't ID the client, he can't ID us either. So zero equals zero. You have a funny feeling about this job? Fine. So do we. It's not the first time. But we're in control. *Capisce*?"

"Yeah, got it."

"OK," she said. "Now, call this big-shot client. Tell him: 'Nobody we know knows whether Kuznetsov is alive enough for us to go ahead, never mind even finding him. We can't do business on that basis. Hire another outfit.'" She ended the call. Drained her glass and poured another fat drink.

She set the bottle in a patch of sunlight falling on the oak dining table. The light passed through the amber whiskey, tracing a narrow line of dark varnish on the wood. Millie noticed that Mary Mike was staring at something in the vicinity of the living room.

Everyone was quiet.

After a moment, Millie said, "I'm going to heat up some of that pizza I saw in the fridge. Anybody want a slice?"

"No, hon'," Mary Mike said, still looking at the living room but seeing something else.

Then Ralph said, "Nah. Maybe a beer." Millie handed him a bottle of Harpoon.

"So that's it?" Ralph said. "We out of this fuckin' deal now for sure?"

"Just a minute, Ralph," Mary Mike said. "I'm thinking. Let me ask you something: What was the weirdest part of that phone call?"

"Weirdest? You kidding? Everything was weird, if you ask me. The fuckin' client, saying find Kuznetsov at the funeral home. What the fuck's he mean? How would the target do that—order in and sleep in one of the coffins?" He paused to chuckle at his little joke. "And then our phone contact in town doesn't pick up? That's never happened before. Boston's the one suppose to contact Barney, then Barney gets in touch with us, right? So somebody's fuckin' with us."

"Millie?" Mary Mike said. "You heard the conversation."

"I heard it, yeah. I saw you go to red alert when Barney told us about the Boston line. Me too. But here's what's banging around in my head—the client telling us to look for the mark at the funeral home. How is that even possible?" She took a bite of the warmed-over pizza.

"What do you mean, dear?"

"I mean," said Millie, "how many people can connect Stepanov and Mirsky with that name? Just the gang that's using the place as a cover-up for murder—except for the two goons who ended up in the freezer. Poliakov, of course, but he's not our guy. So who—one of the gang members playing his own game? Huh-uh. I can't see a motive there. Also, he'd be found out in no time and shot."

"Hey, I just thought of something," Ralph said. "What if the fuckin' funeral home is really the information we been looking for? What Barney said. You think of that?"

"Yeah, I thought of that," Millie said. "And if that's right, then why didn't the client say so in the first place?"

"He had to have a reason for not telling us the other day," Mary Mike said. "But now—I think now he's running out of time. Maybe he's getting worried?"

"Something has rattled him, yeah," Millie said. "He might be sweating a little. So how does all this stuff add up? First: The would-be client knows that Stepanov and Mirsky's operation has been taken over by a Russian Mob.   Second: Somehow the guy's connected, or has inside info. He knows about the phony business with the corpses. And third: He also seems to know that we know what's been going on at S and M."

"How could he know what we know?" Mary Mike said.

"I'm following a hunch," Millie said, "but it makes sense. Why would he tell us that Kuznetsov can be found at Stepanov and Mirsky's? It's because nobody else but us would have a reason to check out a run-down funeral parlor that's recently been the scene of two killings." She paused. "And that means the son-of-a-bitch knows who we are." She took another bite of the pizza. It was starting to get cold.

"I can't see that, Mil," Ralph said. "If this guy gives up S and M as the guy's hideout, what's that got to do with us? Kuznetsov's Russian, the gangsters are Russian—it all fits together. The Russians're the only players on the board."

"No, I think Millie's got hold of something here, Ralphie," Mary Mike said. "Look, why didn't the client just come out and let us know right from the start? I'll tell you why: He didn't want to give himself away, which if we'd found Kuznetsov ourselves and whacked him right off the bat, the client wouldn't have risked coming out of the shadows. Why would we care who he is? It doesn't matter if we know who contracts a hit."

"This guy wants to stay in the dark," Ralph said. "Is that it?" He'd been pacing, his huaraches sounding like crickets.

"He sure as hell doesn't want us to know his identity," Millie said. "If he's hooked up with the Russians, they already know who he is. So what's special about us? Ralphie, would you please sit the hell down? Those fucking huaraches are making my ovaries ache." Ralph lifted both hands: I surrender. He sat down.

"I see where you're going, hon'," Mary Mike said.

"We know something about him that he doesn't want to remind us we know."

"Um-hmm," she said. "We can look at it from another angle, too. Assuming that this bozo knows who we are, and knows that we might know him already, or that we're only a step away from identifying him, what are his options?"

"Looks to me like he's only got one card to play," Ralph said, "and he's done that. He told us, 'Look for your boy at the funeral home.' If we find Kuznetsov and take him out quick, the client don't interest us anymore. He's home free."

"Yeah, that's what he'd probably think," Millie said. "And where does that leave us? What's our next move? What about the phone lines, M?"

"Just a minute, hon'," Mary Mike said. She closed her eyes for exactly a minute. Then took a long pull of the whiskey and sighed—mother's milk. Took a deep breath and let it out.

Millie, not letting Mary Mike off the hook, said, "M, what do you figure? The busy or dead Boston line right after Philly gets in touch with the crackpot client—just a coincidence?"

"I don't know, dear," Mary Mike said.

"OK, but think," Millie said: "There's the primary system, the back-up system, and enough burners to stock Walmart for a year. So the Boston guy had plenty of ways to stay open for business. Not a coincidence, in other words."

"Let me catch up here a little," Ralph said. "What do you mean, Mil?" He had a drink of the Harpoon.

Mary Mike raised the palm of her hand toward Ralph: Be quiet. Her eyes hadn't moved away from Millie, who said:

"Here's the way I see it: The system isn't down. Providence couldn't talk to the Boston guy because Boston was talking to somebody else. The dead line? That definitely shouldn't happen. What if somebody's trying to run a tap?"

Mary Mike stood up. Went to the sink and drew a tall glass of water. She drank it down in a single long swallow. Ralph looked at Millie, and raised his eyebrows—what gives? Millie just perceptibly raised her shoulders.

"All right," Mary Mike said, "we have a situation. I'll run a check. Then I'll get in touch with Lydia Glove. You and I can pay her a visit after supper."

"Did you leave out a chapter somewhere, M? I'm not following the plot. Who is Lydia Glove? How does she come into it?" Millie felt a familiar stirring in her gut.

"Lydia's the woman who runs the Boston station."

"Tha hell...?" Ralph said. "A woman? Why the fuck didn't you tell me this? I'm suppose to be in the know." He crossed his arms, leaned back in his chair. Started to say something else. Changed his mind.

"Another one of your little surprises, M?" Millie said. "What's next—Ralphie's pal over at Dippin' on our payroll too?"

Mary Mike took a deep breath to clear the whiskey fog. "Well, dear," she said, "It's probably just a coincidence, but Lydia's Russian. Her name used to be Lydija Golovna. Now it's Lydia Glove. She might have been a spy at one time, too. Steve Yukovich and her are good friends. He introduced us. Remember Steve, Millie?"

"He helped us find Father Dmitry," she said, "who led us to Stepanov and Mirsky. Who are probably dead. Small world out there—is that what you're saying?"

"Yes, I guess so, hon'. Anyway, after getting to know her, she seemed a good choice for the Boston station. Solid background experience."

"'I'll bet," Millie said. "Hard to beat 'Former Russian Spy' on the lady's résumé."

Chapter 13

Blue Lawns, Wine Dark Sea

Thursday, 7:30 p.m.

They drove south from Newton to Worcester Street. until they hit Linden, then headed southwest to Wellesley. The evening was cool. The big Camaro V-8 growled regally, a big cat waiting for the signal to leap forward. Millie had the windows up: She liked the peaceful, enclosed interior, liked listening to the tires humming against the pavement, the engine throbbing under the hood, Jared PM singing tracks from his new album, *Nice to Meet Me.*

Millie was wearing jeans and black wingtip Thom Browne boots, an English lambskin Dawn Fawn leather jacket that retailed in Milan, Paris, and New York at Oggi/Domani shops for €3,995. She got hers free, compliments of the rage new designer Michele D'Amico, a guy she'd known in high school as Marty Dershowitz.

Funny thing: She'd run across Marty at one of Mandy's agency parties. Totally smitten with Mandy, he'd given her three of the new jackets for modeling his new line. She could have asked him for the Papal Seal—no sweat. But OK, Mandy had also selected the Dawn Fawn, as well as Mr. D's Wine Dark Sea and the Flamingo Flame, a color that only Mandy could get away with because who cares what she's wearing if Mandy Bradford's wearing it?

At first, Mr. D had offered to sell the Dawn Fawn to Millie at half price, seeing as she was an old pal and all. But Mandy took him aside and said, "Marty, Jesus, you and I know that the profit margin on these jackets is criminal, so just give the Dawn Fawn to Millie with love and kisses, and the next time you pass the basket, maybe I'll put a little something extra into it." She was leaning against him, saying these hot nothings into his ear while her hand was rubbing his skinny chest. Thus, Millie's soft, svelte, sinful new jacket to set off her black lambskin driving gloves from Buccioni.

"You're quiet, dear," Mary Mike said. "Is everything OK? I really do like your new car, by the way. It makes me feel—I don't know—safe. It's these rounded seats. You know, I always did like to drive around at night."

Mary Mike was wearing beige slacks, sensible black shoes, a light wool turtleneck sweater—off-white—and a jacket to match the slacks. Her hair was twisted into a bun at the back of her head. Why dress up to see one of the contacts? Millie thought. M doesn't get too many nights out—that's why.

"Hmm? Oh, just listening to a song I like, M," Millie said. "But also thinking it's been a long day and more secrets have crawled out from under the rug. I wasn't the only one who was surprised: You had Ralphie chewing on his huaraches when you told us about Lyudmilla."

"Lidija, hon'."

"Yeah, I know. Still . . ." Millie was easing into the moment, settling into her Zen mode of relaxed awareness, effortlessly taking in everything around her. Like the lights of a car that had been tailing her for at least five minutes, a BMW that had picked them up after they'd turned on to Linden. It was three cars behind her now.

A few minutes ago, it had passed her and then dropped back. Two men in the front seat, the passenger briefly glancing her way. Textbook surveillance, maybe, but easy to spot. Especially since the headlight on the driver's side was canted a bit to the right.

"I'm sure you've been wanting to know why I didn't mention her right away, when we started talking about these Russians," Mary Mike said.

"The thought did cross my mind, M, but then I figured you had your mysterious reasons that I hope won't get me killed some day out in the field." She was driving through posh, quiet neighborhoods now, the streetlights winking on, giving a soft bluish glow to the barbered lawns. Gatsby's blue lawn, she remembered from a lit class. Applying her elite education to practical matters at hand. She turned left, using the turn signal.

"Here's a confession, Millie," Mary Mike said. "I think I just got into the habit of keeping secrets. It's like lying. I mean lying to outsiders, of course, but just the same it's a habit. Protective cover, I guess. It's the job, don't you think?"

"For Christ's sake, M, you don't need protection from me and Ralphie—and save the psychoanalysis for Dr. Phil. By the way, what does this Russian do, aside from forwarding phone messages to us—or is that a secret too?"

"She's retired now. Like I said, there's a rumor that in Russia she worked as a spy. I don't know if that's true. She's had three rich husbands. Two of them Russian. The other one was an American. They all died fairly young—that's according to Steve Yukovich. Mysterious illnesses, he said. It's something she doesn't want to talk about." Mary Mike patted her hair. Licked a finger and smoothed back her eyebrows.

"No kidding. Well, she ought to fit right in with the bureau of state secrets around here. Did she ever do a job for you and Ralph?"

Mary Mike put her hands in her lap. "No, dear," she said, "Lydia just took over for the fella at the Boston station who collapsed in a Southie bar one night and had to be replaced. Oh, look: We're almost at Lydia's place."

The Camaro and the BMW with the canted headlight were the only cars on the street she'd just taken. The other car was sixty yards behind her. In her rear-view mirror she could see the outline of the two men in the front seat. Millie braked, slowly pulled over to the curb. So did the other car.

"Why're you stopping, dear?" Mary Mike said. "Two more blocks, then take a right. She has a big two-story white house, really nice. Steve told me that Lydia paid a fortune for it."

"I know where we are, M. I just want to give you a heads-up. Tighten your seatbelt. Somebody's been following us."

"What? How can that be, Millie?" she said. Mary Mike turned to look back.

"I don't know. I'll figure that out later," Millie said. "There's a pistol in the glove compartment. Get it out and rack one into the chamber. Do you know how?" Millie pulled her Glock from its holster on her hip and a silencer from the magnetic holder under the dash. She screwed on the silencer. The Camaro's engine was still running. Headlights on.

"Jesus, Mary, and Joseph," Mary Mike said. "I haven't shot a gun in years! Hardly ever used them in the field. God help me, I preferred needles." She opened the glove compartment and pulled out a Glock 27, a smaller, more compact model than Millie's 22.

"Maybe you're wrong," she said. "Why would anyone follow us?"

"Why? Are you kidding? I've just whacked two Russian hitters, and by now half the Russian gangsters in Boston probably know that we're looking for Yuri Kuznetsov. Any other questions?"

"If you're right, they'll try to kill us, won't they?" Speaking matter-of-factly, not afraid.

"Probably."

Mary Mike checked the load in the magazine, popped it back in. Chambered a round like an expert. Just like bicycle riding—you never forget.

"OK, M, hang on—let's see if those bozos know how to play," Millie said. She threw the car into gear, floored the gas pedal, and the Camaro, whipping its tail back and forth, bolted forward.

Chapter 15

Driving Lesson

4.5 Seconds Later, 60 mph

The BMW was already losing ground. Millie kept gunning it—80 mph now—but warned herself that this was a residential neighborhood. Her plan: turn left—now!—and keep circling left, staying well ahead of them but not losing them. Find a narrow side street or maybe a cul-de-sac. They'd figure she'd be boxed in, but she'd use that against them.

She got lucky: cul-de-sac coming up. Slowing to 60, she took the Camaro into it, the car bucking as she braked and down-shifted to make the sharp left turn, stopping the car hard at the top of the keyhole-shaped loop. She swung the Camaro around until it was pointed directly at the narrow entrance. The headlights were on high beam. She and Mary Mike had about four seconds, five max, before the hotshots in the BMW arrived.

"Out, Mary Mike! Keep your door open. Get behind it. Shoot anybody who gets close to you. Use plenty of ammo."

Millie leaped out of the driver's side, the engine still running, leaving her door open too, heading for the

88

hedge in the nearest yard. No lights on in the house. She dived behind the hedge, then up in a crouch, moving fast toward the entrance of the cul-de-sac, Glock held down and at an angle. Watery moonlight playing over everything.

She heard the BMW only a second before she saw it skidding toward her, out of control. The driver had waited too long to slow down for the turn, had braked too hard, and couldn't stop the skid and momentum of the car. As she threw herself out of the way, Millie saw the car's right-rear wheel slap against the curb and explode, and she thought the car would roll over. It leaned for a long moment, but fell back. The driver had lucked out, but then he punched the car forward too fast and ended up on the edge of the humped grass median of the cul-de-sac, leaning to the right. He gunned the engine, but the blown tire nearly tipped him over again.

The BMW faced directly into the Camaro's headlights. The driver started up again and tried to back down off the median strip. Dirt and gravel flew. Then the harsh sound of metal scraping against stone—the car had struck a large rock. The driver gave up, killed the engine.

Millie was already there, behind the BMW. She shot out the other rear tire, moved to the driver's side, put a slug straight through his window an inch or two in front of him, and then shattered the windshield with two more rounds. Give both men something to think about. She signaled to the driver to get out. She was standing directly in front of his door, several feet back.

He looked at her but didn't move. His hands were on the steering wheel. Millie got up close, fired another shot in front of him that blew out the passenger window, and said, "Get the fuck out!" To the other guy she said, "Hands on the dash—on top, where I can see them." He didn't move either.

There wasn't time to present a reasoned argument

why it would be sensible for him to comply. She fired a round into the passenger's left arm. He jerked and seemed to spasm: "Uh, uh, uh." His left hand waved back and forth over his buckled seat belt. "Uhh, Uhh."

She pointed the Glock at the driver. "Out. Hands in front of you."

She stepped farther back from his door. He opened it and got out slowly, maintaining eye contact with her, hands held up to his shoulders. The wounded passenger groaned, muttered curses in Russian.

The driver stood in front of his door, facing her. The Camaro's bright lights, streaming from Millie's left, cast long dark shadows of her and the driver all the way to the street. There was no sign of Mary Mike.

"On the ground, now!" Millie said. "Kneel, then lie face down." She watched them both—the stubborn passenger and the slow-moving driver.

The driver dropped to his knees, put his left hand on the ground, eased himself forward, and with his other hand tried to reach into his jacket pocket. He never got a chance to use his pistol: Millie fired two rounds into his forehead.

She knew that the passenger would have a gun too, possibly in the glove compartment, and that he would go for it. She fired three quick rounds his way.

She couldn't be sure where she'd hit him because at the same moment three loud shots rang out. No silencer. Mary Mike. The impact of the bullets slammed the passenger's head violently forward into the dash. A fourth shot followed.

Millie waited a second or two. Silence all around. "Do you think that's enough?" she said.

"You told me to use plenty of ammo, dear," Mary Mike said. "Remember?" They were talking across the top of the car. "I just wanted to make sure." She walked to Millie's side of the BMW. "What do we do now?" She was breathing hard, her voice constricted— surfing on a wave of adrenaline, Millie figured.

"We get the hell out of Dodge. One of these houses is empty, but people in the others are going to be calling 911. Your pistol was loud. You didn't have a silencer."

"You didn't give me one."

"Sorry, we didn't have time to go to Walmart."

Chapter 16

Shattered Glass

Thursday, 7:40 p.m.

The police cruisers, lights flashing, sirens piercing their eardrums, rushed past them going the other way. They'd driven out of the cul-de-sac with seven or eight seconds before the cops arrived. Now Millie was working her way back toward Lydia Glove's place.

Mary Mike was still breathing hard. "God, I need a drink," she said. "Or just a glass of water. I'm really thirsty."

"Just nerves, M," Millie said. "You done good back there."

"Jesus, Mary, and Joseph," Mary Mike said, "I was flying high, I don't even remember running to the car or aiming the pistol. I just saw you shooting the driver and the other guy removing his seat belt, and then I was right behind him firing before I'd even thought about it."

"That's the way it happens. Your instincts take over."

"Then I realized you were shooting the same guy too, and then everything went quiet." Mary Mike sucking in rapid, shallow breaths.

"You OK?" Millie said. They were driving through

peaceful suburban streets again, the soft lights playing down on the broad yards like a scene from "Lives of the Rich and Famous." Mary Mike still had the Glock in her right hand.

"Yeah, I guess, hon'. I'm just not used to this anymore. Wait'll we tell Ralphie, I can just see him." She started to giggle. Nerves again.

They were now on Lydia Glove's street. Her big house down the block was lit up like a cruise ship. She was expecting them.

Millie slowed down. Looked at the place. "Jesus, M, what'd she do—rob the Kremlin? Why does a single woman need a house like that?"

"What are we doing here, Millie?" Mary Mike said. "I can't do this now—meet with Lydia. Sweetie, I really, really need a drink."

Millie pulled over to the curb. Stopped the car to let Mary Mike settle down a bit. The engine was still running. "Relax, take a few deep breaths. Hold each breath a few seconds, then release. You did fine, you reacted like a pro." She paused. "Maybe you ought to put your pistol away, though."

"Oh. You're right." She looked at the Glock for a few seconds. Put it back into the glove compartment. "Fwooo." She let out a big breath. "OK, I'm fine. Mission accomplished. But I'm not ready for Lydia. She's like gangbusters, all hugs and kisses, little pinches, and—I don't know—that big Russian voice. What's one extra day?"

"For Jesus' sake, Mary Mike, you're the one who called this meeting. You know that Lydia could be up to her ass in this thing. She's not gonna try to call us again—it's our move."

"I guess."

"We need to have this meeting. Now. Forget about what just happened. It's nothing."

"Look at my hair—it's all over the place."

"It always is. She'll never notice. Lydia's bound to have liquor on hand. I've never heard of a Russian who didn't have a quart or two of Stoli in the freezer. It's against their religion to drink water." She moved the Camaro out into the street, driving slowly the last fifty yards or so to Lydia's place.

Staying close to the curb, Millie eased ahead, just short of Lydia's driveway. Cut the engine. Opened her door. The Camaro was shaded by a tall tree with a massive trunk and branches—a beech, she guessed. The neighborhood was peaceful and elegant, obeying the iron laws of money.

"Stay in the car," she said to Mary Mike. "I need to check something." She tossed her jacket into the back seat. Closed the door. Mary Mike lifted her hands: What's going on?

Millie lowered herself to one knee, ran her gloved hand under the rocker panel on the driver's side. Nothing. Kept moving her hand under the car, all the way back to the bumper and around to Mary Mike's side. Still nothing.

Millie got back in the car. "There's a flashlight in the glove compartment. I need it."

Mary Mike handed it to her. "Hon', what are you doing?"

Millie didn't answer. She was now back outside, her head down, shining the flashlight along the bottom of the Camaro. She checked every inch. There was nothing to find. The obvious question came to mind: How did those assholes know which car to follow? And an even more pressing question: Who sent them out to kill Mary Mike and me?

She opened the door, pulled her jacket from the back seat, and stuck the LED into the right-hand pocket. When she got back in, she said, "Get your pistol out again. I think Act Two is about to begin."

"Dear, I'm losing track of what's going on. What

happened? What were you looking for under the car?” Mary Mike had the 27 in her hand now.

“A tracking device,” Millie said. “No luck. Somebody knew ahead of time where we were going, when we’d be on the road, maybe the kind of car we’d be driving for all I know. They just had to pick us up on the way.”

“What? How could they know? Oh my God—the phones? That means Lydia...”

“Yeah, that means Lydia, all right.”

Millie drove the car slowly forward, turned into Lydia’s long gravel driveway, rolled past the front door, which was open, all the way to the back entrance of the house. She nodded at Mary Mike’s pistol: “A round is already chambered. All you have to do is fire the damned thing.”

The lights were on in every room facing the street. Light streaming from high poles in the front and back yards. No way to remain unseen, she thought, but there’s no reason to make noise, either. She stopped in front of two tall French doors, each with five vertical rows of three windowpanes. A great bar of bright light spilled out of them on to the flagstones. The doors were part-way open.

Somebody had smashed the pane nearest the door handle. The two panes right above that one had small round holes with spidery cracks running in a concentric pattern all the way to the wooden frames. Glass shards glittered on the flagstones. These panes had been broken from the inside. The one closest to the door handle had been shattered from the outside. What the hell?

“You see that?” Millie said.

“I do. Sweet Jesus. What should we do?”

“Give me a sec’.” Then, a moment later: “Here’s the plan. I’ll turn the car around. Then you’re going to drive back to the street, slow and quiet. You’ll be OK. We haven’t attracted any attention so far.”

“What?” Mary Mike said. And again: “What?”

"Go home. And don't speed. Shoot anyone who tries to stop you."

"Leave you here? I can't do that, dear. What're you planning to do?"

"Just look around. It'll be better if I'm alone." She got out of the car. Walked around to Mary Mike's side and opened the door. "You'll like driving the Camaro."

"Millie," Mary Mike said, "I don't like this one bit. We don't know what's up with Lydia. Somebody might be in there waiting for you. Anything's possible." She grabbed Millie's arm. They were standing by the back bumper, two women holding loaded pistols, facing each other, talking softly in the evening. "I'm not scared, you know. I've just shot a man. So—what do I need to do?" Millie led her to the driver's side. The door was open. Mary Mike slid in.

"When you get home, park the car around back and tell Mr. Moustakas what happened. Tell him to get here ASAP."

"Why don't I just wait around the corner somewhere? You snoop around and then meet me."

Mary Mike paused: "How're you going to get back?"

"You sound just like my mom." Millie eased the driver's door closed, heard it click, then quickly stepped back out of the lights and disappeared into the thick shrubbery circling Lydia's property.

Chapter 17

Bullets Lettres

Thursday, 10:30 p.m.

So what did you do then, Mil?" This was Ralphie. He, Mary Mike, and Millie were sitting at his kitchen table having black coffee laced with bourbon. Mary Mike had had a good start on the others. She'd broken the seal on a bottle of Jack Black a couple of hours earlier. They'd just finished a pizza from Lenzini's.

The streets were quiet. The little kitchen scene was cozy—a family quietly discussing the evening's murder and mayhem.

Ralph was wearing what Mary Mike called his Hugh Hefner robe—thigh-length, burgundy, with black satin lapels. Red plaid drawstring bottoms from J C Penney. His favorite, winter or summer. Mary Mike was dressed in baggy blue plaid flannel cotton p.j.'s that were either L. L. Bean or . . . no, they had to be L. L. Bean, Millie thought. Fresh from a shower, still drying her hair, Millie had on blue jeans and an orange and black Oregon State Beavers sweatshirt, a gift from Mandy in one of her antic moods.

"I didn't want to go in through the French doors," Millie said. "Too risky. So I stayed in the shadows as much as I could while I walked around the yard to check the place out."

"Millie, hon', I really should have stayed with you," Mary Mike said.

"Huh-uh. You always worry about your high blood pressure, and you were already bouncing around like a balloon losing air. I had enough to worry about."

"You figured I'd pop an artery, is that it? You're so sweet." She apparently wasn't being sarcastic.

"OK, OK," Ralph said. "Let's just, will you just give us the details, Mil? What happened then?"

"On my way back to the side with the French doors, I found a body, about forty feet back from the house."

"Jesus Christ, why didn't you say so in the first place? Is that why you wanted Mr. Moustakas?"

"Just listen, Ralphie, OK? I didn't know about the body when I told Mary Mike to call him. I just figured we'd need a clean-up. There'd been a break-in, there were pieces of glass on both sides of the French doors. That wasn't a gentleman caller. There was a good chance that he'd whacked Lydia."

"Sure, I see. So then . . ." Ralph poured a big dollop of bourbon into his cup, added a splash of coffee.

"The guy was face down in the pine needles under a big tree. I got out my flashlight. He had short, dark hair brushed forward. Dark pants. A Haband leather jacket that had been through the mill. The right sleeve had several rips, wrist to elbow. There were two exit wounds in the back. The soles of his boots showed a lot of wear. He looked like a bum, but I didn't think a bum would be sent out as a hitter for the suburbs."

"Jesus, Mil, who cares what the fuckin' guy was wearing?" Ralph lifting a hand from the table, along with his voice. He was leaning forward, toward Millie.

"You want the details, or not, Ralphie?" Millie said.

She took a drink from her mug. "You can tell a lot about people by the way they dress for work, that's all I'm saying."

"What?" Ralph said. "He's dead and you're thinking about a—whaddaya call it?—a dress code for a contractor? Gimme a break." A big pull from the coffee-bourbon mug this time. He nodded his head, sat way back in his chair, waiting.

"I could see that he wasn't an important guy in the organization—otherwise he would have had more money for clothes."

"Meaning what?" Ralph said.

"Meaning they're using players off the bench, Ralphie, not their starters."

"You're saying that maybe they're hurting, with the two you put in the freezer and then the two others that were busy chasing you guys around Wellesley, that're now on their way to the city morgue. That's good thinking, Mil, but I have some questions."

"Ralphie, dear, be patient," Mary Mike said. "The girl is doing her best. It's been a hard night for her. She's giving you a detailed picture of the action. Isn't that nice?"

"Yeah, I appreciate, I'm just saying . . ."

"Do you want her to just say, 'I found a dead guy outside and then I found Lydia in the house with a serious bullet wound and then I went home'? No, you don't want that, you want to know what it was like to be there, so if it ever comes up in conversation, you'll know what to say."

"Sorry I asked." He didn't sound sorry.

"You asked for the details. So Millie's giving them to you." Mary Mike took a good hit from her coffee cum bourbon. "If you ask me, Ralphie, I want to hear every little thing, because I had to leave the party early and missed out. Though I had a big night, I have to tell you."

"Yeah, I get it," Ralph said. "It's just, you come home

hour and a half, two hours ago, needing a drink. You give me this—no disrespect intended—this crazy story about you guys whacking two bozos who'd been chasing you on the way to what's-her-name's house—Lydia's— and you can't sit down, you're all over the place. So I say, 'Jesus Christ, will you just sit down and have a drink and then tell me what happened?' and you say, 'First, I need a shower.' OK, that's fine with me, but ain't I entitled to the details? And on your way out of the kitchen, you say, 'I'm going to take the bottle with me.' And then pretty soon Millie's here and she needs a shower, and I still don't have the whole fuckin' story. OK? So there's a body. How'd he get there? How do you know he's with some outfit and not some jerk with a hard-on?"

"And are you getting the whole fucking story now, Ralphie, while you're still asking questions?" Mary Mike said. "Pardon my French. I'm a little tipsy. But don't worry: I won't start singing 'Danny Boy.'" A big night all-around for Mary Mike, Millie saw, no question. Hearty drinking called for.

"Here's the way it was," Millie said. "First of all, there was a pistol on the ground under the guy's hand. A Makarov. Used to be standard issue for Russian cops and soldiers, maybe still is, but anyone can get hold of one—like those clowns at S and M the other night.

"I sniffed the barrel. It had been fired. I turned the guy over. Two entry wounds in the middle of his chest, four or five inches apart. Nice shooting. The shooter had held a steady hand.

"Then I popped the mag from the pistol. Ejected the round in the pipe. I had an idea: I put the Makarov in his right hand and crossed his hands over his chest, the way I did with the two guys at Stepanov and Mirsky, you remember? Then I took a few pictures of him looking like a saint. His eyes were wide open."

"Jesus H," Ralph said. "You were sending another fuckin' message, right? Like you did at the funeral home. No doubt about it, Millie, I always said you're aces. What was the message this time? Some kind of Russian joke? Help me out here."

She didn't answer him. "Then," she said, "I shoved three live rounds into his mouth. Took a couple more pictures. Squeezed his mouth shut. Then I closed his eyes with my hand."

"Yeah, Mil, you got a great sense of humor. Right, Mary Mike?"

"You were mad as hell, weren't you, hon'?" Mary Mike said.

"What were the bullets in his mouth supposed to say?" Ralph said. "This guy—this corpse—he's saying, the bullets are saying, 'you're next, you son-of-a-bitch, you're gonna get whacked next,' right? The guy's load-ed mouth is supposed to scare those guys, is the way I see it. When the Russkies get wind of this—the same MO, hands over his chest with his gun, plus the fuckin' guy suckin' on loaded cartridges—they're gonna know they're next on the list."

"I have to admit, hon', that's a complicated way to send a message," Mary Mike said. "But I think Ralphie's right." She crossed her arms and squeezed herself.

Millie went on: "OK, how do I know that this guy's at the bottom of the totem pole? The crappy clothes, his ID, and what he had in his pockets. An expired Mas-sachusetts driver's license with the name Viktor Koslov. He had eighty bucks in his wallet. A Visa card. A card for a massage parlor in Miami. It was smudged and folded. The only other thing was a business card in one of his pockets. Try to guess." It was getting late, but she was enjoying herself. You couldn't make this stuff up, she thought. Or you could, but who would believe you?

"Huh?" Ralph said. "How would I know?"

"Mary Mike?" Millie said.

"What a night, sweetie. That's all I can say. It's got to be Stepanov and Mirsky, that's what I think. Otherwise it wouldn't mean much to us." Mary Mike got up, poured the bourbon-coffee mix still left in her cup into the sink, and said, "I'm going to go with straight bourbon now."

"Yeah, that's right: Stepanov and Mirsky," Millie said. "There was a name scribbled on the back. Mary Mike? You're on a roll here. Give it a shot."

"Jesus, Mil, we've almost killed the whole bottle," Ralph said, "and we're still playing guessing games? You know I'm no good at that stuff. Who the hell cares? Those undertakers—that's where they take all the Russian corpses, right? So what if this guy has a business card? Maybe they're trying to build up their trade? Like, 'We appreciate your business.' Or, get this: 'Our customers never complain.'"

Pause. Ralphie laughing at his own joke. Then: "Oh, I get it," he said. "The dead guy had it because he was already planning to whack another poor bastard."

"It was your friend in the embalming room, wasn't it, dear?" Mary Mike said. "I forget his name. I can't keep up with all of these Russian names." She poured the last of the Jack into her cup. "I'm going to open another bottle, Ralphie," she said. "Still the shank of the evening. We all need to relax."

"OK with me, go ahead," Ralphie said. "But where the hell were we? Mil?" He wasn't quite drunk, Millie saw, but he wasn't sober either.

"How I knew that the shooter was a dumb bozo and an amateur. A smart guy wouldn't have broken a pane of glass under so many lights. There were other ways in. Like the kitchen door, which just happened to be unlocked and shaded by an awning."

"So he was dumb enough to get himself whacked," Ralph said.

"Yup. And yeah, Mary Mike, you won the prize again. The name on the back of the business card was Poliakov—Anton Poliakov. I kept the card. You never know."

"OK, I got that far," Mary Mike said, "it's a small world. But my goodness, what does that mean? Who put Poliakov's name there? Do you think he's involved in all of this?"

"Involved? No, I think Poliakov's next on the hit list," Millie said. She poured half a cup from the new bottle of Jack. Suddenly she felt tired. "You know, tomorrow morning's going to be hell, don't you? Meanwhile, poor Mandy will be worried. I should call her."

"No need, dear," Mary Mike said. "I called her when you were showering in the guest bathroom."

"I should go home."

"Without finishing the story? C'mon, Mil. Just wrap it up, OK?" said Ralph. "I still got a million questions."

"All right," Millie said. "What time is it?" She looked at her watch. "Eleven-thirty. OK, I can still get a good night's sleep. But I'm going to switch to beer." She brought a bottle of Sam Adams to the table and a sleeve of saltine crackers. Soak up the alcohol, she thought.

"Lydia got shot too," she said. "You already know that. She's in a private facility or something that Mr. M knows about. She's going to need a good doctor."

"So that nobody knows where she's at, right?" Ralph said. "I bet I know where it is. It's a big house not too far from here, over on the hill. Retired doc with a shady reputation has a basement operating room just for special customers that don't need a lot of publicity. That's the rumor I heard, anyway. Was that the one?"

"I don't know. Mr. Moustakas just wanted to know where to put the body I found outside Lydia's house. Put it on the loading dock at the back of S and M, I told him. 'Make sure the guy is laid out just like he is in the photos I just sent you,' I said. 'Then call the police and the *Globe*.'"

"But here's something I can't get over, Mil—you said that Lydia tried to shoot you when you found her. That's right, ain't it?" Ralphie here, lifting his shoulders, a kid asking his teacher if he'd correctly remembered the lesson. "For Chrissake why? You said it like it was no big deal, but, you know, those're fuckin' bullets flyin' around."

Millie nodded. "She fired off a couple of rounds in my general direction, yeah. Maybe she thought I was there to whack her, but who knows? She was out of her head."

"Where did you find her, hon'?" Mary Mike said.

"I'm getting there, M," she said. "I went in through the kitchen door. A huge kitchen, by the way, with a marble island in the middle big enough for a hockey rink.   No one there, or in the library, or in the small office next to it, which had only a small table holding a laptop and a black leather portfolio. The large living room had beige and blue furniture with white carpeting from one end to the other. It was lit up like a movie set.

"The French doors were across the room from me. On the polished stones in front of the doors I saw big red splotches—blood. It looked like drip-painting, and it trailed across the white carpet all the way to the double staircase in the foyer facing the front doors."

"Jesus," Ralph said. "She was hit pretty bad."

Millie flashed back to a night in the Iraqi desert when she and Pfc. Emmett Ford were pinned down by sniper fire behind a ragged rock wall. He had a bullet hole in his chest and wasn't going to last long. Millie remembered returning fire with her M4, emptying the clip, pounding another one in, emptying that one too.

"It got worse," she said, her voice low, her eyes fixed straight ahead. "At the foyer the red drips became red footprints. Halfway up the staircase to my left I saw Lydia—a tall woman with well-muscled shoulders and a storm of blonde hair. She was lying against the stairs on her back. Blood pooled on a white runner beneath her. The bullet had gone into her gut about three inches left of her navel. She was pressing the wound with her left hand. It wasn't doing much good.   Her eyes were closed."

"You figured she was dying, right?" Ralph said.

"I didn't like her chances. Her feet were bare. Her right foot was full of glass shards. I went up close to get her pistol. She was holding it in her right hand across her knee. She was sweating like hell, and she smelled bad from the gut shot.   Her breathing was shallow, raspy."

"Is that when she tried to whack you?" Ralph again. Mary Mike was listening hard, her eyes staring at the picture in her mind.

"'Lydia,' I said. 'Don't go to sleep.' She opened her eyes. I reached for her pistol with my left hand. She shook her head, pulled the gun away. She said, 'Fuck . . . "and something like 'chetchov' in a hoarse whisper. I figured she meant 'Kuznetsov.'

"Then she tried to lift the gun and aim it at me. I grabbed her wrist and pushed it away. She managed to squeeze off a couple of rounds. They went to the side and blew holes in the heavy glass panels in the front doors. The whole thing was over in a couple of seconds. It was pathetic."

"Jesus, Mary, and Joseph. You were almost killed, dear," Mary Mike said. "I had no idea . . . . I feel terrible about not being there with you."

"I was never in any danger, M. She was too weak to aim straight. If her sight line had been on me, I would have shot her. My Glock was a couple of inches from her chest. I figured she'd be more useful to us alive, if she pulled through."

"I don't get why she wanted to whack you," Ralph said. "Jesus, you were there to help."

"She didn't know who I was. All she knew was that Mary Mike and someone else from the firm were on their way to see her. And remember—she'd already been shot. She probably wasn't in a friendly mood."

"Out of her skull, that's gotta be it," Ralph said. "Who's gonna handle the Boston station now?" He looked at Mary Mike. "You got any ideas?"

"Something's off here, Ralphie," Mary Mike said. "The guy who tried to break in—he got there not long before we did, right? Is that just random chance? And here's something else that's bothering me: He didn't go there to rob her, but to kill her. Why?"

"Hell if I know," he said. "You think she knew she might be a target?"

"If she survives, we can ask her," Millie said, "but when the guy shoved his arm through the glass on the French doors, she showed up with a weapon in her hand. He shot her in the belly, but she fired two rounds into the center of his chest. Pretty good shooting, whether she was hit first or not."

"When did Mr. Moustakas show up?" Mary Mike said.

"A few minutes after Lydia shot her front door. I was trying to stop the bleeding in her side by pressing my rolled-up jacket against it. Army training. I told him where the dead guy was and said, 'We're out of here in three minutes.' I saw that Lydia had passed out, and I went back to the study to grab the laptop and portfolio."

"Who called 911—you or him?" Ralph said. "They can trace the call."

"Me," Millie said. "I used a burner. I told them I was one of the neighbors."

"What the hell did you say?" Ralph again. His mouth dropped open.

"Jesus, Ralphie. What do you think I said? I said, 'Somebody chooting guns ness door, I think.' I was using my finest accent for the occasion, Ralphie. 'And people drivin' all over the place. You know that TV show call *Choot Baby Choot*? Li' that.'"

"All right, all right, sorry I asked," Ralph said. "What were you thinking?"

Mary Mike was smiling, but a little blurry-looking,

Millie noticed.

"I was thinking how mad Mandy's going to be when she finds out that there's blood on my new Dawn Fawn leather jacket that retails for four thousand Euros."

"Tha fuck?" Ralph said. "I don't unnerstand certain things. That's nuts. I know you gals like to dress up, but why wear your fancy clothes when you're going out in the field?"

"I like to look good on the job, Ralphie," Millie said.

Chapter 18

Shampoo

Thursday, Midnight

Back in her apartment, Millie took another shower. It'd been one of those days. Her muscles were still tense. I'll use another one of Mandy's shampoos, she thought. Bottles of Oribe and Bvlgari, a tube of Acqua Di Parma Colonia—total retail cost approximately the yearly GNP of Canada—were all lined up on the tile shelf in the shower.

She turned on the water, adjusted it, stood for a long time under the soothing warmth, the soft-plashing spray flowing down her back. Why did Lydia try to shoot me? Scared? Out of her head, as Ralphie thinks? Why would she want me dead?

Millie closed her eyes, relaxed. The warm water helped. Let the idea bubble up by itself. Don't force it. What's missing from the picture? You know the drill—ask the right questions, and you'll get the right answers. Millie let her mind go blank, trying to lift the pressure behind her eyes. OK, is there a possible connection between Lydia Glove and Viktor Koslov, the guy she shot? And what's the connection between the thugs who wanted to kill me and Mary Mike and the guy who shot Lydia, if there is one?

It wouldn't come. She was too tired to think. Sleep on it, she decided.

She selected the Acqua Di Parma Colonia, which she'd used once or twice before. I'll buy Priss a new tube. She inhaled the subdued, rich aroma, squeezed some of it on to her hand, rubbed it into her scalp, rinsed, and put more on her head. My god, this is good, she thought. Lordy, lordy, my mom used to say. She loved washing her hair. Johnson's Baby Shampoo. No need to spend more money on pricey stuff, she'd say.

Another pair of hands began washing Millie's hair, the fingers rubbing slowly, confidently, back and forth over her scalp. Then the hands were massaging her trapezius muscles, hurting them pleasurably with bold, strong thumbs. Next came the shoulders, the arms, the lats. Millie could feel every fiber in every muscle relax.

Mandy pressed her long body against Millie's back. She wrapped her arms around Millie. No words for a few moments, just touch. Nothing else needed.

"That shampoo cost me the earth, *Tesoro*," Mandy said. She kissed Millie's neck under the earlobe. Slid her hands over Millie's breasts, then slowly lowered them all the way down. "And now you're going to pay a steep price, my fell beauty."

"I know I should have called, Priss, but there was this dead guy that I had to get ready for viewing. Then . . . oh, god," she said, "that feels good. Don't stop. But can you do the trapezius some more?"

"I have two hands, *Tesoro*, not four, but I'll see what I can do. Another long day at the office, then?"

"I had to stay late to send a message," Millie said.

"Yeah, Mary Mike told me. Very danerous, she said. She sounded a little drunk. Did somebody try to shoot you?"

"There was that, yeah. You'll be glad to know that

she missed."

The warm water was sliding over them, a steaming waterfall in their glassed-in grotto.

"And of course the fucking postmortem, right, that couldn't wait till morning?" Mandy said. They were facing each other now. "I love you, Tes, you know that?" They kissed. Kissed again. "Even though you use my shampoo."

"I love you too, Priss. I'll buy you some more, I promise. Something exotic. I heard there's a great product out there called Russian Amber."

"I don't want any Russian stuff that'll turn my hair to straw."

More kissing—coy, playful, sometimes with a little biting. The steam rose past their shoulders, wrapping them in milky mist.

"Have you been drinking, Tes?"

"Bourbon-flavored toothpaste. CVS special."

Then they were drying each other with thick, thirsty white towels. "Now turn around, Priss, and I'll do your front."

"Ummm, that's good," Mandy said. "Keep doing that—no need to rush."

"You shaved for me. I should have spent the night at home instead of shooting people. Let me get your legs now."

"No, go back to where you were." The entire bathroom was warm, steamy, sweet-smelling. The world outside had disappeared. "Who else would I shave for?" Mandy said. "I mean, there's Emerson, and the girls at the agency, but we're all undressed all the time anyway, and . . . oh, Jesus, don't slow down, *Tesoro*, I'm almost there."

"I'm asleep on my feet, sweetie. I'm sorry. Tomorrow morning, OK? First thing. We'll make the earth move."

"Just don't wake up and tell me you have a headache," Mandy said. "God, what I have to put up with."

A few minutes later they were in bed. It was 1:30 a.m. "Thanks for the massage, Priss. Pure magic. I owe you one. 'Night." Millie turned on to her right side. Buried her face in a big down pillow.

"You owe me more than one. Just remember tomorrow morning."

"Mmmm."

"By the way, why did the woman want to shoot you? I'm not clear on that. It was Mary Mike's Russian spy, wasn't it? I would never have trusted her in the first place."

"Mm-hmm."

"You don't know?"

"Hm-mmm."

"Well, darling, for what it's worth, in my admittedly limited experience, if someone points their gun at you and starts shooting, they want to kill you. That's lesson number one. Lesson number two is, there are really no good excuses for that sort of conduct."

Mandy snuggled up to Millie, put her face into Millie's hair. "You smell beyond delicious, Tes. I absolutely want to consume you." Pause. "Did you hear what I just said?"

No reply. Just soft breathing. Millie pulled Mandy's hand around her waist and held on to it.

Chapter 19

Down the Rabbit Hole

Friday, 9:00 a.m.

Next morning. Millie's been awake for an hour, trying to unlock three questions: Are the guys in the BMW connected to Lydia's shooter? What's the link tying them to the thugs at the funeral parlor Tuesday night? There's got to be one. And: Who sent Viktor Koslov to kill Lydia?

She looked over at Mandy, sleeping the sleep of the innocent, one long leg uncovered. Millie lifted the comforter over the leg, tucked the soft cover in a bit. Sex that makes the earth move would have to wait.

One really annoying thing—Millie now reviewing the amateurish way they'd backed into this Russian mess—we don't even have a fucking contract on Kuznetsov and we've produced five bodies. You've iced four thugs, another one is now dead—compliments of Lydia Glove—and Lydia herself is barely hanging on, thanks to Viktor, the dead guy in her yard. And here's the payoff: You still don't see the full layout of this deal, so you're not sure what the next move should be. Perfect.

But there's always a next move, you just don't see it yet.

OK, let's start with the major players, talk to them. Lydia's indisposed, so that leaves Anton, who I hope is still breathing.

She got up, brushed her teeth, dipped in and out of the shower. Drank down a double Alka-Seltzer, followed by a steaming mug of chicken broth, and then a long, slow swallow of bourbon—best way to stay out in front of a headache.

As she pulled clothes from her closet, she again thought back to last night: Why did the guys in the Beemer want to kill me? That's easy—someone who knows I took out the two night-crawlers at S and M wants to get rid of me. But Mary Mike—also a target, or would she just have been collateral damage?

Go back a step. The two guys you whacked and put into the freezer—who did they work for? Their boss will be the guy who sent the men in the Beemer. But how did they know where you were going? Wasn't Lydia the only one who knew that Mary Mike was driving to Wellesley to see her?

Too many things lead back to Lydia—and she doesn't come out clean any way you look at it. But why does someone want her dead?

Millie slipped on a pair of tight dark slacks and her trim black Frye boots with the cross-stitching at the sides. G.I.-issue khaki T-shirt and a black jacket— Alessandra Italian leather lambskin—long enough to hide the Glock, short enough that she could yank the pistol from her holster without a hitch.

She got into the Camaro and phoned Mary Mike. "It's me, M," she said. "Can you text me everything that Philly has sent us? I'm on my way to see Poliakov. We need to have a little chat before he leaves town or another hitter finds him."

"I assume it's after noon, sweetie, otherwise you wouldn't be calling," Mary Mike said. "I haven't opened my curtains yet. I'm afraid to move my head this morning. How's yours?"

"Hair of the dog, M. Couple of Alka-Seltzers and then a bite or two of Jack Black—you'll be fine. Look, can you also dig up some shots of Kuznetsov's pals, gang members, guys who've done time, girlfriends, business cronies, anything— whatever you can find. Also some photos of Lydia."

"Oh, honey, you want this stuff right away, don't you?"

"M, you could find George Washington's underwear on sale at Macy's if we wanted it. Call your freaky computer wizard in Toronto if you need help." Millie ended the call.

She pulled into the drive-thru at a Starbucks. Gave Anton a call. Five rings before he picked up. "Yes," he said, "is Poliakov speaking. I am asleep not long enough." He hung up. She called back. Six rings this time. What the hell's the matter with that guy?

"Flat white grande, three shots, whole milk," she told the intercom when it was her turn.

Anton finally answered. "Is not Poliakov. He is leaving town ten minutes ago."

"Goddammit, Anton, don't you know who this is?" She paid for the coffee, pulled out onto Storrow Drive heading downtown. The traffic was light.

"Yes, I know," Anton said. "Is the lady assassin. I am in enough trouble, please. Soon I will be gone."

"Yeah, you told me—Utah, to join the Mormons."

"That was maybe crazy idea, I think. Now I have other plans. I call my cousin in Kyiv. He tells me, 'Come back home, Anton. We need you to fight Russians.' I tell him, 'Sergei, I am fighting Russians here in America. I want quiet life.' So he say to me, 'You want buy farm and raise pigs, *tupoy*?'"

"*Tupoy*? Do you like pigs?" Millie said.

"Means dumb-shit. No, I dun like. They have bad smell. And is slop everywhere. I am no good with animals. Sergei knows this. He says, '*Zhopa*, that was joke. We must kill Russian invaders now, before Kyiv falls. You must come home.' So I return to Kyiv now."

"Jesus, Anton, you're going to be a Ukrainian soldier?"

"Yes, why not? I am Ukrainian Russian."

"I have trouble seeing you carrying a rifle, that's all. Right now, though, you and I need to talk. It's important, so listen up. Pack a bag and take only what you need for a long trip. You can't stay at your apartment anymore."

"I am in danger, you are saying. Is not a surprise." Millie imagining him nodding his head. "But who wishes to kill me?"

"I'm trying to figure that out," she said. "Are you using one of those burners I gave you, by the way?"

"Yes, I use burning phone. You are only number, so I know who calls."

"And the call to Kyiv? Did you use your iPhone?"

"No, I buy new burning phone at Valamart. Then I throw away."

"Ten minutes, Anton. Don't be late. Same corner as the other day."

Millie pulled on a black baseball cap and a pair of dark glasses. Force of habit.   The shades were Tory Burch and had set her back $165. They were worth every penny, with lenses large enough and dark enough to hide behind yet sexy enough to draw attention.

Ten minutes later she picked up Anton a few blocks from his apartment. He looked like a refugee with his baggy clothes and battered suitcase.

They drove to a luncheonette that wasn't usually busy at 9:30. They sat in a back booth, Millie facing the front door. She'd finished her Starbucks and was in considerable need of more caffeine.

She liked the old-fashioned feel of the place. Half a dozen booths on one side, a long bar on the other. A cylindrical glass case on the counter with individual pie slices stacked inside.

Two men sat at the bar eating breakfast. One of them reading the *Globe*. A booth in front was occupied by two young women with backpacks. Students, probably, but they didn't seem to be in a hurry to get to class.

"You are afraid of sunshine?" Anton said. He pointed to her dark glasses. A wiseass this morning, despite the likely danger. Trying to cheer himself up. Good, he needs it. Anton was pale and unshaven, his electrified Einstein hair streaming in all directions, gravity pulling at the double bags under his sad dark eyes. A natural-born worrier if she'd ever seen one. Maybe it was a special talent some people had, like ESP or whistling two notes at the same time.

The waitress arrived, took their order. Bacon, three scrambled eggs, whole-wheat toast for Millie. And a mug of coffee ASAP. For Anton, just tea with sugar and lemon. "I am no good to eat Amedican breakfast," he said. "I am too nervous."

"Just a sec'," Millie said to the waitress. "You're not hungry?" she said to Anton. He shrugged his shoulders. Millie ordered bread and butter for him, raspberry jam, a fruit bowl, and sausage.

He looked at her. "You have maybe some Russian in your blood? Still, I am not hungry."

"Suit yourself," she said. Then she ran through the high points of last night's events. Anton's forehead crept up, but he sat completely still. When she came to the Stepanov and Mirsky business card, with Anton's name written on the back, Anton closed his eyes and nodded his head. "They have plans to shoot me, yes? I am dead man. Please tell me why."

Their meals arrived. Anton pushed his plate to the side. "I cannot eat. My head is breaking. You must help me." His voice the sound of someone in a deep well. The two young women in the front booth got up to leave. They were laughing about something. One of them did a high-energy booty shake for the other. I'll have to tell Mandy.

Between bites, Millie laid it out for Anton. "You're probably next on their hit list, Anton. You know too much about the crooked business at Stepanov and Mirsky—that's why they want you dead."

"Yes, I see," he said. "I am never going to be soldier with my cousin in Ukraine."

"Don't worry," she said, "you might still get away from these guys. They can't use the hitter who got Lydia. He made too much noise breaking in and got shot."

"And she is expecting someone?" He took a bite or two of the fresh fruit.

"I don't think so—not a shooter, anyway. She was expecting me and a friend of mine. She had something important to tell us."

"Yes? This lady is assassin too? Her business is like yours?" He drank some of his tea. Leaned over the table to get his answer.

"No, but I think she was a Russian spy at one time, and she knows how to handle herself. She knew enough to shoot the guy who'd come to kill her."

"But her enemies—they are looking for me? I have no spy secrets." He ran a hand through his high-voltage hair. She couldn't tell whether he was being bleakly ironic or naturally paranoid.

"Let's go back a little, Anton. I'm trying to get some things straight. Your bosses are gone. Mirsky left in a panic a few days ago. The other owner—Stepanov— hasn't been around for weeks. You were hired, and bodies have been mysteriously piling up since then. A few of them are legit, but most of them are unidentified guys with fake death certificates. Courtesy of the Russian Mob—no other logical explanation. Am I right so far?"

"You are asking me why this happens? I know nothing."

She put her hand up. "You know that somebody gave you a corpse that you thought was Kuznetsov. You prepare it and send it off to be cremated. Turns out the guy was somebody else. Now you've got a problem."

"Yes, a problem. I remember. One of many."

"And then," Millie said, "another guy who was supposed to be Kuznetsov shows up. As you said, a popular guy. Only his real name was Popov, right? At first you thought it was Podolsky, but it was actually Popov. So you checked with Mirsky: 'What're we supposed to do?' You're in uncharted territory."

"Mirsky calls this guy Boris to ask what to do, yes," Anton said. "Mirsky shits his pants to talk to Boris. Every time, he is afraid. This time, Boris tells him, Popov now must be called Kuznetsov on the death certificate. 'OK, OK,' Mirsky is saying. He can barely talk. Two minutes later Mirsky runs away." Anton now nibbling at his bread and butter.

"And you're left holding the bag."

"I know nothing what's in the bag." He had finished his tea. Millie flagged the waitress. Pointed to their empty mugs: another round.

Millie waited until the girl had brought fresh coffee for her and another pot of hot water and a fresh tea bag for Anton. "In Russia," he said, "tea is stronger. Is black. In Ukraine too. Here, is like colored water. But I don't complain."

Millie's phone pinged. Mary Mike. The photos. There were six of them. Two of the individual shots were mug shots. The third and fourth, taken with a telephoto lens, looked like surveillance photos. There were also two group shots from newspapers. They didn't look very recent. There were no captions.

"I want to show you some photos, Anton," she said. "Maybe you can identify one or two of these people." She decided to start with one of her own snaps of the dead shooter under the pine tree. "Ever see this guy?"

He looked at it. A slight shrug of the shoulders.

She moved to the next one, a close-up of the shooter, mouth closed over the bullets. "How about this one? Do you recognize him?"

Anton glanced up at her, then down at the photo. "Yes, I see him. Viktor, he is called. Is errand boy for Stepanov, I think. They dun tell me. He brings body to us one time with no papers. Two times, he takes away empty casket. He dun ask me. He just takes. Do you shoot this man?" He had finished his bread and butter.

"Nope, somebody else did. The spy I told you about. Two rounds in the chest. Tell me about him. What else do you know about him?"

"Is pretend tough guy. He walks like big shot in your Hollywood movies. The others who work for Stepanov make fun of this man."

"The two that we put in the freezer—they were Stepanov's men?"

"Yes, Stepanov's men. They dun like this guy. He has no respect. He is also crazy, a little. Explain why this man goes to her house to kill the woman." Anton took a big pull of his tea.

"That's what I'm trying to find out. Why would anyone want to assassinate her? At this point I'm guessing it's Stepanov. He sent Viktor. But why?"

"So you are asking me. You think: Poliakov is Russian, so he will know how these things work. I know nothing of this business," he said. "Is all a mystery to me. But I am afraid—like poor Mirsky. Already people are trying to kill me, and what do I know? Nothing."

The waitress returned to their table. "Can I get you guys anything else?" A tall girl with a long brown ponytail, chewing gum. Pleasant smile. Big brown eyes.

"No, thanks," Millie said.

"Okey-doke, you want the check then?"

"Yeah," Millie said.

"You know, if you don't mind me sayin'," the waitress said, "those dark glasses are super. They're fire. You get 'em online? I have to tell you, though, I lose every pair I get. But I'm gonna try to hold on to these." She pulled a pair of wobbly Dollar General shades from her tiny waitress apron. Under the apron she was wearing a threadbare green and white checkered gingham dress with plus puff sleeves. It barely reached her knees. She said, "I'll be back with the tab in a sec'."

Millie turned to Anton: "I have a few other photos for you." These were the shots Mary Mike had sent her. The first mug shot showed a youngish, studious-looking, round-faced man with neat black hair and startled eyes behind wire-framed glasses. The lettering beneath the shot: DMITRY PESKOV. What the hell? she thought. This is the same guy we called at the church to ask about the funeral? He's a priest now? Huh-uh, not likely. But what if he's passing himself off as a priest for some unknown reason? Think about it. Why not?

"Does this guy ring a bell?" she asked Anton.

Again he shrugged, but this time he turned his head to one side and frowned as well. "No, is nobody to me."

The second mug shot was a real beauty—a guy with gold front teeth and a massive jaw who looked like one of the stone statues on Easter Island with poor orthodontics.

"I never see this man," Anton said. "I would remember."

The third guy—a surveillance photo—was the one who'd back-handed Anton in the parking lot the night they wheeled the corpse into the mortuary. A bitter smile appeared on Anton's face. "Yes, he comes sometimes with Stepanov, to deliver death certificate to me. Now is dead, I dun worry about."

The waitress brought the check, gently pressed it down on the table, and silently walked away.

"One or two more, Anton. Then we're out of here," Millie said.

She pulled up one of the black-and-white group photos Mary Mike had forwarded. A picture of Kuznetsov with friends—five people at a party, sitting in a curved booth in a restaurant with drinks in front of them. Two women, three men. Kuznetsov was sitting in the middle. Mary Mike had circled his image. Millie guessed from the dresses the women wore that the photo was at least half a dozen years old. One of the women looked familiar.

"Do you see anybody you recognize?" she said. Anton studied the photo. He moved his head a little, this way and that: maybe, maybe not. "Let's open it up," Millie said. She stretched the photo with her fingers, told him to take his time.

"Yes, this is Stepanov," he said, pointing to the man in the middle of the booth. He had a big head and a thick, brushy mustache. "Is long time ago, but, yes, is Stepanov. Had then more hair."

OK, Millie, be careful here, she thought. "After you went to work at the funeral home," she said, "how many times did you see this guy before he left Boston? Didn't he leave when they hired you?"

"He leaves, yes, but later, maybe three, four weeks. I am not paying attention. Stepanov shows me how to fix the papers to match bodies."

"The phony documents."

"Yes, but at first I dun understand. He says to me, is the way to do things. What do I know?" He had finished his bread and butter and most of the raspberry preserves. Not bad for a guy who wasn't hungry.

"Do you recognize anyone else in the photo?" she said to Anton.

"Is maybe Stepanov's wife or girlfriend," he said,

"the woman who sits next to him. I see her in office with him one day. Signing papers."   Anton pointed to a tall woman next to the guy. She had broad shoulders, blonde hair pulled back in a bun, and a dark spaghetti-strap dress with perilously low cleavage. She had her hand on his. The rpm's inside Millie's chest were accelerating.

Millie had expected Anton to recognize one of the other men—maybe—but not one of the women. And for sure not this woman.

"How do you remember this stuff all of a sudden?" Millie said, excitement in her voice. "You've never mentioned it before."

"Is not all of a sudden," he said. "You never ask me. Is not important to me the night those *zhopas* put me in cooler. We are finished now, yes?" He had eaten the Russian breakfast Millie had ordered for him, but he still looked burned-out and nerved-up.

Lady friend or wife—it makes as much sense as anything else does in this bat-shit case, Millie thought. She flicked her phone to pull up one last shot. Same group, same party, better angle of the woman and the guy Anton had identified as Stepanov.

"Here she is again, Anton," Millie said. "Do you want to change your mind?"

"No," he said. "Is same woman. You see birthmark on the arm?   I see when she comes to funeral home. She dun like me to look. She tells me, 'What the hell you are doing up here? You are supposed to be downstairs carving up bodies, yes?' Then laughs Stepanov and closes office door to me."

Yes, Millie saw the birthmark, which was covered in the first group photo. It was not new to her. She had seen it last night when its owner had pointed a pistol at her.

Millie took a closer look at the photo. She noticed an image off to one side of the people in the booth. The figure was partially obscured by shadow, but she had no doubt about who it was.   Bending over to listen to the guy sitting at the left end of the booth was Dmitry Peskov, smiling with one side of his mouth, his smooth round face turned toward the camera.

It's down the rabbit hole, Millie thought, with no bottom in sight.

Millie left a big tip for the waitress. She scribbled a note on the back of the bill: "For you. Try not to lose them." The Tory Burch glasses rested on the note.

Chapter 20

Till Death Do Us Part

Friday, Noon

There's still some stuff I'm not real clear on," Ralph said.

"Like what?" Millie said.

They were in Ralph's kitchen eating a special Irish lunch that Mary Mike had prepared—corned beef sandwiches, cheese and ham toasties, sausage sandwiches. Ralph, for his part, had filled the fridge with Bass Ale and Guinness Stout, which he was mixing half-and-half to make Black and Tans. Millie was starved, even though she had eaten breakfast only a couple of hours ago.

"Like, why did you take Poliakov to a dumpy motel, anyway?"

She had dropped Anton at a semi-shabby two-star Motel 6 where she figured the Russians wouldn't sniff him out, and then burned rubber back to Continental Removals on Cabot Street.

In the motel parking lot, Millie had told Poliakov, "Ask for Miss Dorine and tell her that Auntie sent you. You can trust her."

"Yes, and what do I ask of this Miss Dorinya?"

"Just say you want to get to Ukraine right away and have nobody follow you. She'll do the rest."

"I do not understand the rest," he said, "so how does she know to help me?" His left hand was squeezing his grizzled chin.

"Anton, I'm in a hurry, so pay attention here. She'll ditch your refugee ensemble and buy you some jeans and a gray hoodie so you'll fit in with everybody else. She'll give you a clean shave, cut your hair short, dye it, and arrange for a new passport. That'll take two or three days. That's it."

"But I have passport now, valid for yet a long time." His hands were now squeezing his knees, his voice a sine curve of volume and pitch.

"We're not going to take a chance that the Russians will find you. The new passport's your ticket out. Choose a new name—something bright and cheery, like Gleb or Igor." Trying to lighten his mood a bit, but not getting anywhere.

"I am here lost and now with headache." His eyes were bright, milky saucers floating behind his wire-rimmed glasses. This is what shellshock looks like, Millie thought.

"You'll be fine. Give Miss Dorine this envelope." Millie reached across Anton's legs and pulled a fat tan envelope from the glove compartment. She plopped it on to his lap. He nodded his head.

"Is money, yes? You have to pay this lady to help me?"

"Jesus, Anton, don't be so thick-headed. Her services cost money. She's not going to get you out of the country safe and sound just because she thinks you're pretty."

Millie got out of the car, took Anton's ratty suitcase out of the trunk, and set it down on the concrete. It sagged like a half-deflated balloon. Anton just stared at it—a mysterious object dropped from a low-flying spaceship.

"A final suggestion, Anton—work in the military's medical corps. Your experience at Stepanov and Mirsky will be a big advantage, and you'll probably live longer." Before Anton could reply, she was back in the Camaro, the car fish-tailing as she roared away.

Now, back with Ralph and Mary Mike, Millie said: "Ralphie, that Motel 6 is run by Mary Mike's old pal Dorine Fogg, who's an expert at helping people get out of Dodge—don't you remember?" She took a bite of her cheese and ham toastie, washed it down with the bottom half of her Black and Tan. She closed her eyes—Christ, that's good.

"Oh, yeah, yeah," Ralph said, "the one that got Louie Fortune into Canada just ahead of the Feds that time. The dumb shit was brought back soon after that, so it didn't do him any good."

"It wasn't Dorine's fault," Mary Mike said. "Louie came to her in a sweat, 'Get me a new passport impromptu and presto'—you know how he talked—but Louie, he never thought things through. The U.S. has an extradition treaty with Canada, so he was back home and behind bars before he could unpack. He had a new passport, all right, but he kept the old one for back-up, and he happened to use it when he checked into a Toronto hotel." She washed down this long speech with the hero's portion of her beer.

"The tight son-of-a-bitch couldn't throw anything away," Ralph said. "But let's go back to something else here that I don't get. Why did Kuznetsov pretend to be Stepanov? He could've just forced Stepanov to run the mortuary as a front man."

"We don't actually know if he used that alias," Millie said, "though my gut tells me he did, at least for a while. All we know for certain is that Poliakov identified Kuznetsov in the photos as Stepanov, the head guy he worked for in the mortuary."

"What do you think was the big payoff for impersonating Stepanov, dear? Who'd even care who ran the mortuary?" Mary Mike said. She was slicing a corned beef sandwich into triangles. Her glass was empty. She caught Ralph's attention, handed the glass to him.

"Remember that Kuznetsov faked his own death a couple of weeks ago," Millie said, "and the *Globe* reported it. Then Mirsky hightailed it when some guy named Boris ordered him to ID a corpse as Kuznetsov. And tomorrow there's going to be a funeral for a guy named Yuri Kuznetsov, who's alive and well. So whatever his reasons are, he sure as hell wants to stay in the shadows."

"And the *Globe* article—we know that wasn't fake news, right?" Ralph said.

"Yeah," Millie said. "The *Globe* just got it wrong. So did the cops. They were all taken in."

"So Kuznetsov was alive then, and he's alive now, and he was never dead, is that what you're saying?"

Millie glanced at Mary Mike, closed her eyes, shook her head slightly. "That's right, Ralphie, he didn't die, and he didn't come back from the dead. I'm proud of you. He's just hiding out."

"OK, OK, I was asking for that," he said. "I'm just keeping the details straight in my head, that's all."

"He's probably just steering clear of his enemies," Mary Mike said, "that other Russian gang that the *Globe* mentioned. But it could be he's dodging the FBI too. Maybe both. If everybody thinks he's dead and gone, he's home free. He can take his money and vanish."

"Makes sense, M, if anything makes sense with these guys."

"Yeah, I see, Mil, but this Russian bullshit is so fuckin' complicated," Ralph said. "How do you manage to figure anything out?"

"I'm just trying to make all the pieces fit together,

Ralphie. Sometimes I get lucky. Look, Stepanov's been dead for quite a while, OK? For how long, we don't know. People believed that he was away on a long vacation in Florida, but the vacation was strictly a long sleep in a cheap coffin. Kuznetsov probably iced him when he took over the business for one of his scams. My guess is money-laundering."

"Easier to whack the son-of-a-bitch than explain the facts of life to him, right?" Ralph was building three fresh glasses of Black and Tan. He was careful, deliberate, an alchemist conjuring up a layer of gold, then a layer of dark brown, and finally, at the top, an inch of celestially white foam.

"At that point," Millie said, "maybe he thought, what the hell, Stepanov's dead, I'll just step into his shoes for a little while and avoid unnecessary publicity."

"Yeah," Ralph said, "and he had a perfect place to dump the bodies his mugs stacked up. His guys show up at the mortuary with a stiff, put it in a box, no fuckin' questions asked. Pick up the fake death certificates. Burn or bury the corpses, there's no evidence of a crime." He took a big pull of his Black and Tan, then gazed raptly at the glass.

"Look," Millie said, "maybe this stuff is useful, maybe not, but I nearly lost an ovary speeding back here to talk about Lydia, see how she figures in this damned tangle. We know she's in the middle of it all somehow. You've seen the photos. She's with Kuznetsov, or used to be. I gotta admit, that threw me—head of the Boston station an old friend of a Russian Mafia boss. Then, a few days ago somebody—we don't know who, though the number of candidates is shrinking—asks us to ice Kuznetsov, and last night that very same Kuznetsov sends out a shooter to whack Lydia. If you believe this is all a coincidence, hold up your hand."

"You're pretty sure the hitter was his guy?" Ralph said.

"Oh, yeah, everything points to him," Millie said. "The thugs that chased M and me in the Beemer, the S and M business card with Poliakov's name on it that the shooter had in his wallet, and the big thing—his mission to take out Lydia. There's only one guy who could pull all those strings. Kuznetsov."

"I agree, dear, and I have an ugly suspicion or two about Lydia, to boot," Mary Mike said.

"They're married—is that it?" Millie said. "I knew it."

"They're married, all right," Mary Mike said. "We came across a copy of the marriage certificate in that fancy leather folder that you took from Lydia's house. Dated only six months ago. She didn't even tell us—probably because she's been peddling our secrets, or maybe giving them away for love. She sold us out, pure and simple. And now somebody's got to deal with her." Mary Mike's voice was low, but it felt to Millie as if she was drilling through armor. Mary Mike held out her glass to Ralph—another refill.

"I've always told you," Ralph said, "love and business don't mix, like you and that Wall Street guy you had to put away some years back, guy you found out was cheating on you with his wife after you and him had been using the honeymoon suite at the Ames for months. He crossed you, so then—this is the part that gets me—you dress up like Nurse Betty or Little Red Riding Hood or something, meet lover boy in his hotel room, and jab a loaded needle in his neck. Out like a light, you said—no struggle, no fight, no time for bad feelings."

"There were plenty of bad feelings for me, Ralphie, but sticking that needle into him made me feel better."

"If he'd just kept the wife secret, none of this would have happened, right?" Ralph said.

"Well, dear, he never mentioned her to me. I found out just by coincidence. But it was the reason poor old Andy had to cash in his chips."

"I wonder what secret Lydia's been keeping from

Kuznetsov," Millie said. "Married only a few months and then he tries to assassinate her—looks like the couples therapy didn't work."

"She could have ended up on a slab at Stepanov and Mirsky's joint, just like the others," Ralph said.

"Don't forget about the bank accounts we found, Ralphie," Mary Mike said.

"Which accounts exactly, M? Care to share the news with me, or is this a trade secret?" said Millie.

"Dear, we were just waiting for you to get here to tell you what we dug up. Between those two they have a boatload of money stashed away. The laptop you found at Lydia's? We cracked it."

"How'd you do that?" She slid her empty glass across the table to Ralph.

"We had a little help from our tech guy in Toronto, Avery Plum. Took him about fifteen minutes. Bottom line—Kuznetsov has a couple of numbered offshore accounts, Lydia has one. She also has a bundle in Deutsche Bank here in Boston."

"So where are you going with this?" Millie said. "Do you plan to break into these secret accounts?"

"No, dear, I don't think so, but the idea has crossed my mind. I'm just telling you what we found."

"As his wife, Lydia can get into to Kuznetsov's accounts, you know," Millie said. "She could also do that as his widow. She probably knows how."

"Oh yes, she knows how. She has a list of the documents the banks ask for before they let you transact business in those accounts. We've got that far ourselves, but why would she want to do that? She has a fortune of her own. Why would she steal from her husband?"

"The husband that wants her dead, is that the one you mean, M?"

"Um-hmm."

"The one whose funeral is tomorrow?"

"Yeah."

"I feel like Poliakov, I'm getting a fucking headache from these Russians. How much money does she have in Deutsche Bank?"

"A little over two and a half million," Mary Mike said.

"Christ," Millie said. "You're right—she doesn't need to rob her husband. If he even had a sniff of what she was thinking about," she said, "that'd be reason enough to whack her—motive if I ever saw one."

"Figure the guy has a ton of money stashed away, OK?" Ralph said. "And for this lady, maybe it got to be a big temptation. A character like Kuznetsov, that killing's part of his fuckin' business, he'd have to show how big his balls are and, you know, pow!—take out the wife."

"Um-hmm, it could have worked that way," Millie said, "theoretically. But how would she find out that Kuznetsov, who I don't imagine goes around sharing that information, has money in secret accounts, anyway?"

"Well, dear, they're married, and she's a smart cookie, so it was probably easy to find anything she wanted," Mary Mike said.

"Yeah, I wasn't thinking, plus her graduate degree in the spy business wouldn't hurt either," Millie said.

"Like I said," Mary Mike said, "Lydia wrote down the documents she'd need—proof of citizenship, for instance—and important dates, like his birth date and the dates of recent transactions, which I think you probably need to initiate a new one. She knew what she was doing."

"She was serious, all right," Millie said, "but she was nuts if she figured she could kill a Russian Mob boss and get away with it." Millie drank some Black and Tan, set her glass down, then picked it up and drained it. "She'd have an escape plan, wouldn't she? She'd need to get away right after the hit."

"We located that too," Mary Mike said. She walked into Ralph's office and returned with the laptop. Opened it and turned the screen toward Millie. Lydia had air-line reservations for a trip to Brazil—Boston to Miami, Miami to Rio de Janeiro. The reservations were for one passenger, a woman named Tatiana Petrovna.

"We haven't found a passport with this name on it," Mary Mike said, "but I'm sure Lydia has one."

"Kill the guy, change your identity, empty his bank accounts, and live happily ever after in Rio," Millie said. "You got to give her credit. She leaves the country, no one ever sees her again."

"But her plan backfired," Mary Mike said. "I think she'll probably die instead."

"Um-hmm, the bullet that the hitter fired into her. How's she doing, by the way? Has Mr. Moustakas checked on her?"

"He says she's not doing so hot," Mary Mike said, "but she can talk a little. I might pay her a little visit soon."

"What's the date for the flight out of Logan?" Millie said. She looked at the laptop screen. "Monday—Delta 1674, 4:22 p.m. Two days after the funeral. OK, then, the funeral proves Kuznetsov's dead, and Lydia leaves the country as what's her name—Tatiana. One thing doesn't really add up, though—why bother with the guy's money if she has plenty of her own?"

Ralph suddenly sat up. "No, you're right—it don't add up. I don't buy it—this whole fuckin' story. This crap about the bank accounts, plus the ticket out of the country—what does that tell us except she's running away from the son-of-a-bitch that tried to whack her? She found out about it and decided to get the hell away—that's all."

From Ralph, a pretty strong speech, Millie thought. She saw the point of it, but there was a flaw in his thinking. "Ralphie, that's what bothered me, all right. But remember this: She didn't know he was out to kill her until the hitter arrived and started firing at her."

"Yeah, fuck it," Ralph said. "Maybe we're barking up

the wrong tree here. What difference does it make to us if she wanted his dough or not? It's not gonna change the way she ends up now."

"M, why did you ever hire this damned woman?" Millie said. "Remind me. Just because she had sexy credentials as a spy?"

"Well, Millie, Steve Yukovich knew we needed a replacement for the Boston station and told me about Lydia, her background as a Russian spy and so on, which made her a possible for the job. They were friends. I trusted Steve. He knew that we were in the removals business and wouldn't have recommend just anyone. But we screwed up, didn't we?"

"Problem is, you didn't bring in someone we know," Ralph said, "somebody's kid, like Barney Halcovage in Philly, that you know his mother, or a friend from the old days that we trust from his past history. You were in too much of a hurry."

"And you agreed to it, Ralphie, but yeah, it was my fault," Mary Mike said. "Now what—are you going to shoot me?"

"No, I'm just sayin' . . . "

"Look, what's done is done," Millie said. "We're just trying to get a handle on this thing. Let me ask you this, M—what was Lydia's reason for taking the job? I never asked you. Did she know ahead of time what kind of business you were in?"

"Umm, I don't really know," Mary Mike said. "Maybe. But when she and I started talking, I had to give her a hint or two, you know, and she seemed interested. I remember that she smiled when I laid it all out for her. I wasn't afraid that she'd tell anyone, not after what Steve told me about her."

"Which was what, exactly?" Millie said.

"I already told you, hon'. There was the spy business, which I thought was kind of classy and meant that she'd be professional and keep secrets. She had money from her three dead husbands. And she seemed to have plenty of time on her hands. Also, I could see how smart she was."

"Oh, yeah, the dead husbands you told me about on the way to her house—let us not forget them," Millie said. "Died tragically before their time, left her all their money. The whole thing was hush-hush—she didn't like to talk about it."

"Right, the whole subject was off-limits."

"OK, she clearly didn't take the job for the money she'd earn with us. You've seen that mansion in Wellesley, all those bedrooms, the furnishings that make the Kardashians look poor."

"Who are those people?" Ralph asked.

"They're nobody, Ralphie," said Millie. "My point is that she didn't need a side-hustle, that's all. She must've had another reason to come to work for us. She's been with us how long now—couple of years, maybe a little longer?"

"That's about right, hon'."

"OK, and we know that she and Kuznetsov have been together a lot longer than that, right? The photos prove it."

"Um-hmm. What are you getting at, dear? Ralphie, please fill our glasses, I'm dying of thirst."

"Just a thought I'm playing with, M, following the string. When she took on the Boston station, she'd known Kuznetsov several years—long enough to know that he had a pile of money. Long enough to decide to kill him for it, if you want to think along those lines."

"OK, I buy that—there you have a possible motive for wanting him dead," Ralph said, "but you just said the money from the job didn't interest her, and she has plenty of money herself, so what's the play here?"

"I'm not sure, Ralphie, just let me think a minute," Millie said. She took a big pull of her beer. Paused a moment. "You know, I think Lydia took us for a ride.

She fooled us. That's the only thing that makes sense to me. When the job at Continental came her way, she saw a big fat opportunity and grabbed it."

"Wait a minute, Mil. I'm a step or two behind."

"She'd been planning to kill Kuznetsov for a long time, I assume," Millie said. "The job gave her the perfect chance to take out husband number four. I bet she couldn't believe her good luck. There was no way we'd ever suspect her."

"Ralphie, get down the bourbon," Mary Mike said. "We'll chase it with the Black and Tans. Now, Millie, lay it all out nice and clear for me. My thoughts are a mess, and I don't want my blood pressure to go up any higher."

Ralph brought three tumblers to the table and filled each one half-way up with a fresh bottle of Buffalo Trace.

"Here's what it looks like to me, M," Millie said. "We figured Kuznetsov's money couldn't logically be a factor, but what if it was the whole point? Lydia doesn't need the money to live on—no argument there—she needs it because she's a wacko, a psychopath. Think of the three husbands who conveniently died young and left her all their money—too damned sad for words, can't bear to talk about it, *nyet nyet*. You know what they call a woman like her?"

"Mother of God, they're called black widows, right?" Mary Mike said.

"Yeah, women who kill their husbands for their money. The real spider sometimes eats the male after they've mated. Probably not on Lydia's menu."

"This whole thing, start to finish, is totally crazy," Ralph said. "We never shoulda stuck our noses in it."

Mary Mike had polished off her Buffalo Trace. She took a deep breath through her nose and let it out slowly. "I'm feeling a little better. Sweetie, go on with your story. I just wish that Sister Immaculata could be here. She always said don't trust appearances."

"Somehow I doubt that she'd have this in mind." Millie said.

"With Sister Immaculata you never knew."

"So Lydia, when the time was right, she offered us a contract on Kuznetsov, right?" said Ralph.

"Um-hmm." Millie.

"And we didn't have a fuckin' clue who the client was?"

"Um-hmm."

"We'd take him out, and she'd never have to touch the son-of-a-bitch."

"Um-hmm."

"She'd disappear with his dough, and no one would ever know, including us."

"That was the idea, yeah," Millie said.

"So Lydia's the mystery client—who the fuck could've guessed?"

"We should have, but we missed the clues," Millie said. "Remember when the client was getting antsy and sent Philly the message about Kuznetsov—'He's alive. Try the mortuary'? No one else but Lydia could have known that. We should have twigged, but we didn't."

"And we still don't have a fuckin' contract," Ralph said. "We ought to go into the charity business."

"We're OK, Ralphie," Millie said. "I'll see if Kuznetsov's at his own funeral tomorrow. Maybe he'll be there to celebrate."

"What the hell good does that do, Mil? We can take him out, but how do we collect? Your spider woman's odds aren't too good at the moment."

"Don't worry, I have a plan."

"You do, huh? OK. Make sure you collect double for all the crap she put us through."

"I don't think so."

"What do you mean—how much're you thinking then?"

"About two and a half million dollars."

Chapter 21

Bad Habits

Saturday, October 8, 11:00 a.m.
Funeral for Yuri Kuznetsov, Saint Nicholas
Church

Millie saw right away that the two nuns were going to be trouble.

They entered the church, paused, and looked around before they walked toward the altar. They didn't look like any nuns she'd ever seen, unless convents were recruiting basketball players these days. They were tall and had broad shoulders. In their habits they looked like giant bats with folded wings. They had long arms that extended past their sleeves. And they had hairy wrists.

Millie was sitting in the shadows, as far back as possible, at the end of the last pew on the right. The two nuns walked right past her. They strode down the center aisle, pulled their pistols from under their habits, and began firing.

The nuns worked methodically, shooting everybody in the first two pews on the left side facing the altar—the family's side. Then they turned and walked into the vestry on the other side of the altar. A few seconds later, Millie heard two more shots.

The two mourners on the visitors' side of the aisle had been ignored by the killers. They rose from their seats and double-timed it out the exit at the front. They made no sound. They didn't notice Millie.

She was the only one left inside. She was aware of the faint smell of gun powder mixed with the musty odor of the church rising from its worn-down carpets, its tattered cushions saturated with human sweat, the cleaning wax used to polish its old wooden pews.

The nuns were goons from the Russian Mafia gang Kuznetsov had been running from, Millie figured. One gang attacking the family of a rival gang at a Russian funeral mass in full daylight. It seemed unnecessarily complicated, she thought, dressing as nuns. Why not just walk in and do the job? After all, they knew where the victims would all be seated at one time, and they'd make sure there would be no survivors. Millie decided, though, that the nuns' outfits were perfectly in keeping with the grotesque absurdity of the whole Russian affair.

She replayed the action in her mind—the nuns calmly shooting everyone in the two pews nearest the casket, then walking into the vestry and firing two more rounds. Those were for the priest, Father Dmitry.

What would these guys do next? She moved quickly toward the altar, her hand on the Glock in her canvas tote, her eyes checking all the shooting lanes and angles.

And then she saw a wreath of flowers fly out of the open casket, followed by an arm reaching straight up into the air. Millie saw the corpse sit up, watched as he struggled to get out of the casket. The casket wobbled, fell off its metal stand, and tumbled down on the man, pinning one leg to the floor. Millie glanced toward the vestry for a second, then back toward the man. He struggled to his feet, stared for a moment at the bodies in the pews, limped across the sanctuary, and disappeared behind the altar. She got a good look at him: Kuznetsov, with way too much makeup on his face.

I knew it, Millie thought. I knew that son-of-a-bitch wasn't dead.

Millie pulled the Glock from her bag. Screwed on the silencer. Turned toward the victims: no one moving. Quick and merciless, the work of professionals. A babushka, one other woman, six men. One of the men was only about twenty. Two of them were heavy-set and wore black leather coats. Bodyguards. At least there were no kids.

The gunmen wanted to whack everyone in Kuznetsov's family to show people that their boss—whoever he was—was not a guy you could reasonably fuck with. Fear as the ultimate business policy. Millie guessed that Kuznetsov's gang was now probably wiped out.

She had an idea, then lost it when she heard the police sirens—background music for murder. She turned her head. Behind the altar she saw dark paintings of saints and martyrs.

She was holding the Glock down at her side, slightly behind her leg.

The hitters obviously figured that Kuznetsov was dead, she thought, or they'd have put a few rounds into the casket. Who in his right mind would think that a live guy would be hiding in a funeral casket?

These thoughts took three or four seconds as she stood in front of the altar. Another second or two for her to conclude that the nuns with the hairy wrists were not going to leave through the vestry. They'd have to return this way. She took a deep breath through her nose. Held it. Released.

So she wasn't surprised to see two priests walking out of the vestry door toward her. They were wearing black cassocks, unbuttoned—they'd dressed in a hurry. She recognized one of them from a photo that Mary

Mike had sent her—Kuznetsov in the restaurant booth with people he knew. The guy in the photo had been talking to Kuznetsov. It had looked like a serious conversation. I'll bet it was, Millie thought.

The sirens were about two blocks away now.

"You are family?" the priest she recognized said to her. The two men stopped about ten feet away. "We hear shots while we apply to Father Dmitry the vestments. And now we are here, sadly, to examine the tragedy."

He looked at the overturned casket. "What happens to Kuznetsov?" He made the Orthodox sign of the cross, the one that goes backwards. The other priest just looked at her. He had baggy, sad eyes and needed a shave. Millie knew what was coming.

"You are family?" the first one repeated, raising his voice and his eyebrows and leaning his head forward. The other priest put his right hand under his cassock.

She fired before he could get his pistol out, drilling him at the base of his throat. Before his eyes closed, she put two rounds into the other one's chest, just where a heavy cross should have been hanging by a chain. Then she made sure of the first guy with another shot as he went down on his knees.

She moved toward the altar.

Thinking: How far ahead of me could Kuznetsov be? Would someone be waiting for him? Probably, yeah. The driver of the hearse, waiting for the dead guy to rise up and call for a ride. The driver would have moved the hearse from the front of the church to the rear before the service started. He'd want to be ready for his passenger.

Pretty interesting, Millie thought, this whole crazy case. Wheels within wheels, Mary Mike would say. Lydia's plot was to scram with Kuznetsov's money, but he had a plot of his own set in motion. Think about it: You're the corpse in the casket. You get carried out to the waiting hearse after the priest hands you off to God. Then you and your driver disappear with all your cash and offshore accounts. No one's the wiser.

A great plan, but Mr. K hadn't figured on the hitters.

CHAPTER 22

Closing Time

Saturday, 11:15 a.m.

Millie moved quickly behind the altar, pistol held high in her right hand, steadied by her left. She found a flight of stairs to her right that led to the basement but knew that Kuznetsov wouldn't have gone downstairs—the cops would be swarming the place in a matter of minutes. He must have slipped out through the side door a few steps away.

The door opened at street level. She put the Glock into her bag, pushed the door open, and walked to the broad alleyway in back. There was no hearse, engine idling, waiting for the living dead man. But at the far end of the alley, turning left, pulling out into traffic, she saw it—a Cadillac hearse, 1950s vintage, tail fins, whitewall tires, the whole nine yards. Jesus—a clapped-out funeral car with white walls? Well, it shouldn't be too hard to follow.

The Camaro was a block away. She jogged to it but wasn't in a big hurry. There was only one logical destination for the hearse—the mortuary.

It's possible, Millie thought, that they'd ditch the hearse somewhere between the church and Stepanov and Mirsky's in Milton. But where do you park it without drawing attention? At Star Market? Logan International long-term parking? And how then would Kuznetsov get around with that limp?

No, they'll stick with the plan. She headed to the mortuary and got there a few minutes before they did. She had just parked at the side of the building, out of sight, when the hearse, bouncing on its ancient springs, drove in and pulled up to the loading platform.

Millie watched from the corner of the building. She saw Kuznetsov in the passenger seat and the shadowy head of the driver next to him.

Suddenly there were two quick, loud gunshots, and the shadowy head disappeared.

Kuznetsov opened the passenger door and got out slowly, leaving the door ajar. He was carrying a revolver. He pulled a handkerchief from his pocket and wiped his face, smearing the makeup from the mortician's cosmetologist and the blood spatter from whoever he shot. For a moment he stood in the afternoon sunlight, gazing upward. Then he limped to the rear entrance, where bodies were unloaded.

Millie was just seconds behind him. She saw him walk down the dim hallway and open the door to his right—the embalming room. A tiny shard of light glinted off his pistol. What the hell, she thought, isn't there a better place to rest in this building? Find an unoccupied casket upstairs, treat yourself to a cushy nap?

Pistol at her side, she followed him. Through the window of the embalming room door she saw Kuznetsov, blood spots on his chest and right arm, sitting at the small table where she had first met Poliakov. He was pouring himself a drink from a bottle of Stolichnaya. Of course—the freezer where the cadavers are kept, the perfect place to store vodka.

Kuznetsov looked up and saw her, no surprise on his face. "Come," he said. "Have drink with me." He beckoned with his left hand. On the table next to the bottle lay the revolver, an old .357 Magnum.

Millie pushed the door open.

"I expect my enemies to send someone, but not so soon," he said.

She walked in, her pistol pointing at him.

"You see, I do not hold gun," he said, "there is no need to worry." The Russian accent was there, but it didn't have sharp edges, as if he'd sanded a rough board to make it smooth.

She kept the Glock pointed at him.

He stood up slowly, both hands raised. He turned, brought another glass from the counter behind him, sat down again, and filled it halfway with Stoli. Pointed at it with the bottle: for you.

"No thanks, not during working hours."

"Ah, Amerrican humor." He rolled the r's. "Good." He looked at her Glock. "You are here to kill me."

"Yeah." She moved a couple of steps to her right. Now she had a good view of both Kuznetsov and the door. She crossed her arms, her left hand cradling her right elbow, the Glock pointing only a few degrees left of Kuznetsov's chest.

"Bad place to die, this fucking room. Do you shoot the others, my men who find peace in the freezer?" The accent now more pronounced, curling around his words. Feeling the moment of truth, Millie guessed.

"Yeah."

"Is good joke on them. I appreciate. Where will you place me? I am too heavy for you to lift. Do you wish me to crawl into the freezer to help you?" He laughed. "I see you like to smile too. It is too bad we meet in these fucking circumstances." He drained his glass. Filled it again. "Russians—we drink too much vodka. But makes life bearable."

"Are you ready?" Millie said.

"You are in hurry? You have date?" He seemed genuinely interested.

"I'm just impatient. Why stretch it out?"

"Why? All day I talk with idiots. Savages. They fill me with disgust. Now comes someone with brains to exchange a few words." He took another drink of the Stoli. "My wife—Lydija—she pays you? You have contract?"

"Yes and no. She wanted you out of the way, but we couldn't find you. We didn't know Lydia was in the picture until someone complained to us about her phone. We found her at home Thursday evening, shot by a hired gun. His body was out in the yard. He had two bullet holes in his chest."

"And she is dead too?"

"Probably, by now. She was shot in the stomach and badly wounded. You sent the hitter, didn't you? Viktor Koslov. You also sent a couple of goons to kill my friend and me on our way to Lydia's house in Wellesley."

"I hear Lydija and your friend talk on phone. I know what I must do then. Lydija wishes to kill me. So I send that piece-of-shit Viktor to kill her. He dies. You and your friend I am not acquainted with, but I cannot risk. Is too bad. A great shame. You kill those two in the car also—Sergei and Boris?" The full-on Russian accent now breaking through.

"Yeah."

"I hire wrong people. You are better." He shook his head.

"You had Lydia's phone bugged," she said.

"In my business you are always suspicious. Wife is no different. She gets crazy two, three months ago. All day what she talks about—my money. How much I have, where do I keep? I have housekeeper put bugs in lamps, under tables, in phone. Lydija keeps second phone secret, but we find three days ago and put bug. That way

I know everything she thinks."

"You didn't live with her?"

"No. To sleep with, OK. To live with—impossible."

Closing time, Millie thought. Time to end it. Just one more question.

"Why did you kill your driver?"

"Stepan?   He says, 'Yuri, give me my share, OK? I do everything you ask.' I tell him, 'I have no more men but you. I am alone. You must stay and help me.' 'OK,' he says, 'but give me my money to put in safe place for later.' I see he lies to me, so I shoot."

"Finish your drink."

"Go home. I will do your work for you. I have gun." He waved his hand: Leave me.

She looked at his revolver. He'd do it, he'd shoot himself. He has nothing left.

He looked at her. "Go. I am tired." He waved his hand again, his voice the sound of a man at the far end of a long tunnel.

But she angled the Glock at his chest and fired two rounds. They blew him backwards, knocking him over, the chair clattering under him. His eyes were still open when she walked out the door, but there was no light in them.

Chapter 23

Just Do It

Sunday, October 9, 11:30 a.m.

Christ, Mil, you're telling me the two shooters wore nun's outfits? That's like the bank robbers in *The Town*—you remember—they dressed up like nuns too. Your guys just come in blasting and finish off the rest of Kuznetsov's gang, right?" said Ralph.

"A couple of the victims were relatives, like the old lady. I don't think she was a gang member."

"Yeah, I guessed that, but why the hell go into the church to shoot the fuckin' gang in the first place? In *The Godfather* Michael Corleone had his enemies shot outside the church. Remember that baptism scene? He's inside with the priest, renouncing the devil. His shooters are on the sidewalk or street somewhere taking down the other gang. Nobody had to dress up like nuns."

"What can I say, Ralphie? Life isn't always like the movies. I was as surprised as you are. I was only a few feet away when those goons pranced down the aisle and started killing Kuznetsov's people. But I didn't think of

The Godfather or *The Town*. Obviously I should have. I'll take notes next time."

"OK, good, you're being funny, but it's a good question—why go to all that fuckin' trouble?"

Ralph, Millie, and Mary Mike were sitting in his kitchen at the old oak table eating Dippin' Donuts with coffee. They were doing the postmortem on the Russian case, which had taken them on a roller-coaster ride for almost a full week. It was drizzling outside. The wind was gusting.

Ralph was wearing loose brown slacks and a short-sleeve beige Tony Soprano shirt with two wide brown vertical panels in front. Mary Mike had on a blue daisy-print maxi dress. White mules on her feet. Her hair was in a Kathryn Hepburn up-do style that looked like a bird's nest. Millie wore a pink Nike short-sleeve cropped top and black running tights. She'd just finished her five-mile morning run. She was relaxed, enjoying the postmortem, the warm kitchen.

"Another thing I'm wondering about, Mil," said Ralph, "is why you decided to shoot that son-of-a-bitch anyway, if he was gonna do the job himself?" He took a chocolate donut and looked at it, then put it back.

"Ralphie," Mary Mike said, "this was just a job, not one of those old movies where the woman does something she'll be sorry for later on and you want to scream at her to use her head in the first place, OK? Who knows what the man would have done if Millie had left him alone?"

"She said he was gonna do it, right? Kuznetsov was gonna whack himself. Case closed. It woulda been simpler to just leave."

"Ralph, sweetie, what if he changes his mind? Then what? Does Millie go back to the mortuary and try to find him? Look at it this way: The way she handled it, we get paid fair and square, and nobody gets cheated."

"What the hell," Ralph said, "we were gonna get paid either way. You and Steve Yukovich, you guys set up that power of attorney stuff, so what's the fuckin' difference? You already had Lydia's money locked down."

"The reason I shot him—why should that bother you?" Millie said. "That was the whole story of this batshit week—find Kuznetsov and take him out."

"I don't know, it doesn't make any damned difference. Mary Mike's right, I guess, but—"

"But you want more. OK, think about this, Ralphie. He tried to have us killed—Mary Mike and me—remember?"

"Yeah, I know, I know."

"Two guys in a fast car tail us on our way to Lydia's house. It was clear what they had in mind. Mary Mike and I belt up and drive like hell to outrun them or maybe set them up. We get lucky and trap them in a cul-de-sac and gun down the bastards. M was right there with me, firing the little Glock like a pro."

"I was so nervous, dear," Mary Mike said, "when you gave me that pistol. You know I prefer needles. But out there in the open, of course, you can't just rush up to someone and say, 'Roll up your sleeve.'" She giggled. "Mother of God, my blood pressure that night. I thought my head would explode." With both hands she fluffed up her hairdo.

"That's why I sent you home," Millie said. "You needed to calm down. Ralphie, would you please pass the donuts?" She helped herself to three—two old-fashioned with chocolate icing and one plain glazed.

She turned to Ralph. "Then there's the little matter of tapping into our phone line. That's Lydia's fault—no question about it—the famous fucking Russian spy. Kuznetsov told me that she'd started acting crazy a few months ago. Couldn't stop asking about his money. So he had the housekeeper bug the place."

"Did you say the housekeeper, dear?"

"Yeah. Keep that in mind next time you call Merry Maids."

"Sweetie, I do my own housekeeping," Mary Mike said.

"The woman was one of his plants, right?" Ralph said.

"Yep," Millie said. "Just a few days ago they discovered the Boston station phone—the one she kept hidden—and bugged it too."

"Bingo," Ralph said. "Game over for Lydia."

"Yeah, she's toast from that point on," Millie said. "When Mary Mike phoned Lydia Thursday and said we needed to check for a possible leak on the phone line, Kuznetsov was listening in. He was already paranoid about Lydia's pestering him about money—now he was convinced that she wanted to kill him for it. Why else would she be using a secret phone? That's how he figured it. He decided he'd take her out first."

"OK, but why did he want to whack you and Mary Mike that night?" Ralph said. "He didn't know anything about the contract Lydia tried to put out on him."

"Think about it, Ralphie," she said. "After Mary Mike's call he immediately sent out a hitter to shoot Lydia. But M was the one who had made the phone call. He'd think M probably knew something that could put him at risk. And I was her driver. We were wild cards, unknowns. He was in too deep to take any chances. So he told the guys in the Beemer to kill us."

"These guys must've been pros—they knew which car you'd be driving."

"I've thought about that, Ralphie, and I'm not sure how they did it. But it wouldn't have been too hard to guess our route to Lydia's house if they knew where we started from. M, I remember you told Lydia what time we'd be at her house. Did you say anything about being at Cabot Street?"

"Lydia asked how long it would take to drive there from here. She knew where we were. She started to talk about it, and I told her to clam up that damned second, she was violating security. I knew then that she couldn't be trusted. I was furious."

"Jesus, Mary Mike, you never told me," Millie said. "You should have said something. We were targets from the start." She drained her cup. Set it down hard on the table. "Can I get some more coffee here?" she said, maybe enjoying the postmortem a little less than she had a few minutes earlier.

"It took me a while to figure it all out, dear. I'm sorry. At the time all I could think about was what needed to be done that evening. I didn't know that Kuznetsov was listening in."

"Forget it," Millie said, "nobody knew. The power of attorney—how did you get her to sign it?"

"When you were in that church playing with guns," Ralph said, "Mary Mike and her chum Steve from parochial school days, they—"

"I'll tell it, Ralphie," she said. "I called Steve and explained the situation. 'You know what, kid,' he said, 'I never believed that fucking spy story of hers. I smelled fish from the beginning. I'll be right over.'"

"But you had to persuade Lydia to sign the document, right?" Millie said. "What did you say to her? And the doctor—did he have to weigh in too?"

"Mr. Moustakas let his crooked doctor know that we were going to transfer Lydia to another place. The doctor didn't care. He was being paid plenty to help us. Steve and I showed up while you were shooting those fake priests, and I told Lydia that we'd take care of her from now on."

Ralph freshened up Mary Mike's coffee and offered her the donuts. She took a plain glazed, dunked it, and ate a couple of bites. She nodded her head. She was taking her time. This was her big moment, Millie knew.

"Did she buy your story?" Millie said.

"I don't know, dear, I don't think so, but the doctor said that signing the paper was just a formality for being released. Lydia kind of shrugged and then signed. She had to be propped up with pillows to use the pen. After Steve and the doctor witnessed the document, I asked them to leave the room. I leaned over and whispered to Lydia, 'We did what you wanted. He's dead. And now you're dead too. Nobody leaves the firm.'"

"Sheila's Rule," Millie said.

"That's right, hon'," Mary Mike said. "From the minute we found that passport and the one-way airline ticket to South America, I knew I'd have to kill her."

"Jesus H. Christ, you didn't tell me about this part," Ralph said. "What happened then?

"Lydia's eyes popped open and she started to say something, but I had the needle in her neck by then, and she never said a thing." Mary Mike was breathing hard through her mouth, like an athlete who'd just run a mile. Ralph's mouth was open too, but he wasn't breathing.

Millie turned to Mary Mike: "Where's the body now?"

"I don't know, dear. Mr. Moustakas took care of it. That's his specialty—cleaning up. But it'll all be legit— death certificate, burial, everything. Maybe he'll have her cremated, he didn't tell me. Mr. Moustakas will see to it that no connection between Lydia and Continental Removals exists."

The rain had let up. The sun was shining. Millie watched a bird flapping her wings in a puddle of water in Ralph's yard.

"What does the death certificate say?" Millie said.

"It says she had a heart attack," Mary Mike said. "Coronary thrombosis."

"I have to give you credit, M—you and Mr. Moustakas worked out all the details," Millie said. "Who's going to be the new Boston station guy?" She had eaten the last donut, a blueberry glazed.

"Get somebody we can count on," Ralph said, "you know, that we can trust, like Barney there in Philly. Or that Southie guy that his mother busted his balls to become a famous fighter—Casey Reagan, I think it was."

"His mom told me that Casey's head had been scrambled in the ring—that's how she put it. Poor boy. No, Steve Yukovich is going to do it. Nobody's better. I should have asked him in the first place."

"I got a question, Mil," Ralph said.

"For Jesus' sake, Ralphie, I thought we were all done here. We're out of donuts. I've got to shower and get ready for a date with Mandy. We're going to supper at George's Passing, then we're going to watch some movies in bed."

"That's the restaurant that you get a slice of steak and half a potato for a month's pay?"

"Live large, spend big, Ralphie. Life's short. What's your question?"

"Life's short, yeah, I'll remember that," he said. "OK, getting back to when you whacked Kuznetsov—I know you're gonna jump on me for this, but did it even cross your mind to, you know, let him do it?"

"No, I just shot him, Ralphie—simple as that. I wasn't thinking about anything, except aiming straight. I wanted to make dead sure the job was done right."

Acknowledgments

Sincere thanks and appreciation to Aagje Ashe and Kris Krishtalka for valuable suggestions as I wrote and revised this novel. And to Martha Masinton, my wife, thank you for your editing, which is always brilliant and sometimes even magical.

About The Author

JERRY MASINTON, an emeritus Professor of English at the University of Kansas, is the author of two critical studies—*Christopher Marlowe's Tragic Vision* and *J. P. Donleavy: The Style of His Sadness and Humor.* He has also published numerous essays on modern and contemporary American literature. From the mid-1970s to the mid-1990s he reviewed books for *The Kansas City Star*.

He and his wife Martha, an editor and former publisher of technical journals, head up a writing group in Lawrence, Kansas, called Write-On. They have two daughters, nine grandchildren, and two great-granddaughters.

Wrong Man Down is Masinton's first novel. It is followed by *Dead Sure,* featuring Millie Henshawe, the tough, gay, super-cool assassin who works for Continental Removals, LLC in Boston, a niche firm with a very specialized clientele. The Millie Henshawe series is marked by dark humor, complicated plots, punchy dialogue, and an original cast of characters.